The Infallible Heart of Andy Tiernan

(And why it took me 13 days to get home)

By
Frank L Kress

Thanks Dave,
For all the encouragement, advice, compliments and
critiques

A few words before we begin:

If you happen to be a young person of today, or even an old fart from yesterday, I'm compelled to tell you that reading books is very important. You may think that you can get all the knowledge you need out of video games, but it's just not enough. Sure, video games can teach you how to breathe through your mouth and maintain a glassy eyed stare, but you might find yourself in a situation where mouth breathing and staring isn't enough. Do you think those skills alone will carry you through college? Good point, they probably will, but books are nice too, and you should read them.

Books are filled with all kinds of knowledge. For instance, I came across this tidbit in a book: Did you know that if a man cuts his finger in Des Moines, Iowa, a great white shark swimming in the middle of the Pacific Ocean can smell that blood within fifteen seconds? That's why they call sharks the vampires of the sea.

OK, that's not true. But you gotta admit, that would be a pretty cool name: Vampire of the Sea. That whopper of a lie that I just told you holds an important lesson too – never believe everything you read in books. Most of it is a pack of lies, especially math textbooks. Do they really expect you to believe that a man is leaving Los Angeles by plane and another, completely different man, is leaving New York, also by plane? As if that would ever happen.

But this book is different. Everything in this book is true, and not only that, it's also chock full of fun and adventure. How is that possible, you ask? Well, it's magic. Yes, magic, the one sure thing that you can believe in. It's magical in the sense that when you're like, ninety years old, you can say, "I remember reading that book, and that's magical, because I can't remember my own name! I'm senile!" I'm pretty sure that this book is magical for other reasons too, but if I told you about all of them, there wouldn't be any mystery.

If you're using this novel for an upcoming book report or something to pass the time while you're waiting for a plane, let me congratulate you on your choice. This book is perfect for you. First of all, it's pretty short, which is always a plus, because we've all got better things to do with our time (video games, for instance). Also, your teacher (or pilot) won't give you any flack about curse words, because there aren't any in this book. To be honest, they did occur. Some of the characters cursed a blue streak but I managed to keep it pretty clean. There may be the odd one thrown in there, so if you do find one, don't include it in your book report. Teachers (and morally upright pilots) frown on those sorts of things. On the down side, there are a few big words thrown into the mix. Don't be discouraged if you don't know what they all mean. It's important to have a good vocabulary because if you're like me, you want people to think that you're smarter than you really are. Big words are good for that.

I digress; I do that a lot by the way, so get used to it. So anyway, it's my great pleasure to introduce you to the wonderful and inspiring novel entitled, "The Infallible Heart of Andy Tiernan". The purpose of this book is to provide you, the young person of today (or old fart of yesterday), a book of such character and wit that your life will be radically changed within ten minutes of reading it. It's almost a fact.

OK, once again, that's not even close to being true. I'm just toying with you, because aside from being a minutely talented and average looking writer, I'm also a big fat jerk. But don't let that stop you from enjoying this book. It really is a true story and you could learn a few valuable life lessons. Like you should always be nice to the ugly kid, because no matter what your mom says, you may very well be one of them.

There are a whole bunch of other lessons too, but again, where would the mystery be if I just spelled them all out for you? The answer is that there would be no mystery. But that's the last time I help you out. The rest you have to figure out for yourself.

Day One

Sunday the Tenth

You will often meet with characters in nature so extravagant that a discreet poet would not venture to set them upon the stage.

- Lord Chesterfield

I didn't set out to have an adventure. I don't think that adventures are the sort of things that people can plan to have in the first place. They just sort of happen and nowadays, they don't happen too often. They belong to the world of Tom Sawyer, Huck Finn, and those kids from Stand by Me. What with extreme sports and exotic travel destinations, people set out on adventures all the time but what they usually get is just an adrenaline rush which isn't the same thing. Adventures are spontaneous; they're thrust upon you like the flu virus or something.

Also, I didn't set out to change my life either, which is another thing that people plan on all the time. Most of the planning occurs on New Year's Eve and then most of the life altering resolutions fizzle out around February. At least that's been my experience. Still, what I'm saying is, I didn't set out to have an adventure or to change my life, I only set out for the grocery store.

Whenever I go shopping I'm reminded of all the things that are wrong with humanity. I think of those things mainly because I'm in a building with other members of humanity, forced to observe them in all their puerile glory. Not that I'm some kind of misanthrope or anything. I don't hate everybody. I might, if hatred didn't take up so much energy. The truth of the matter is that I'm much too lazy to hate anyone. People only aggravate me. I have enough vim and vigour to be aggravated, as long as I take regular naps to keep up my strength.

One of the things that really annoys me about people is that they'll believe most anything, and on that life altering, adventurous night, seeing all those people at the grocery store reminded me of one of the great modern myths that has absolutely nothing to do with my story but is thrown in here because, well, it's my story and I can do whatever I want. The myth that sprang to mind was that a grocery store is a great place to pick up girls.

I guess the rationale is that since members of the opposite sex are wandering around with grocery carts, that plenty of opportunities exist whereby a guy can just walk up to a great looking woman and say something like, "I always squeeze the melons." Some kind of witty conversation is supposed to follow and then the two can retire to the produce aisle to act out a connubial preamble among the rutabagas.

Stuff like that almost never happens. It's one of those bills of sale sold to the type of people who glean life lessons from sitcoms and soap operas. They're the ones who go to the store and shop for love and they're easily spotted. There's the older housewife in overdone blush and lipstick bidding her time in front of the dairy foods, waiting for a Tom Cruise look-a-like to sidle up with a basket filled with exotic foods (rutabagas for instance). He'll give her a hot look of lust with dark smoky eyes and in a raspy whisper ask the woman if she'd like to come over to his place for oysters, champagne and you know what. Honest, those pathetic weirdoes are there, and next time you go the store, take a look for yourself.

In the real world there's only one Tom Cruise and he doesn't go to grocery stores. In fact, there aren't even any grocery stores. They've changed to mega super food and drug outlets. There are thirty two aisles and beside the butcher and bake shop is a flower outlet, coffee bar and delicatessen all under one roof; lit up by glaring fluorescent lights and decorated with little red squares that all proclaim the new gospel of "Sale." There aren't any good-looking people doing the single scene in there. The place is full of overweight slobs and snot nose kids running around with red stained hands and lips. Did you ever wonder how kids get those stains? Personally, I think it's the blood of unwary babysitters.

It would be a long and fruitless lecture if I were to list all the modern day grocery horrors. I sum it up by thinking that if the great philosophers walked down these sparkling aisles they would have written a grimmer prognosis for the nature of man. Nietzsche could pause at the checkout counter and mutter that God is dead, and we have starved Him to death with low calorie salad dressing.

I suppose the only good thing about grocery stores nowadays is that they're open till ten at night and you can go when the annoying kids that mothers drag around are snug in bed dreaming about sugar plums and fairies and how to tick off adults in public places.

Despite being waylaid by acerbic thoughts, I managed to find all the items that were on my mental list. I needed shampoo, soap, deodorant and razor blades. It seems that all my toiletries always run out at the same time and when I go to join humanity in public I look and smell just as bad as they do.

So there I was blending in at the checkout, reading the trashy magazine covers out of the corner of my eye. I always do it surreptitiously lest anyone should think that I am even remotely interested in celebrity diets or the Olsen Twin's latest battle with cooties. I only read the stupid things because I get bored standing in line. When I was younger I used to look at what other people were buying and try to see if their purchases gave any kind of clue as to what they were like. It wasn't too hard to figure out that a guy buying Preparation H and canned prunes was not a happy man. I used to be young and naive and I actually thought that people weren't all the same. I guess I'm just a disillusioned old man now.

Before I go on with my fabulous tale I should pause here and let you know a little bit about myself. My name is Zachary Kinfleisich. As you can well imagine, I was teased about my name all through school. I was mostly referred to as King Flea Itch.

Kids are so witty and imaginative that I wish I could give them all a great big hug in a giant vice.

I'm twenty-two years old and I'm writing this during an unscheduled sabbatical from University. I'm midway through my third year and I have yet to pick a major. I tried a few different things but it seems that the only thing I have an aptitude for is drinking espressos and smoking cigarettes. I was at a bit of an impasse as far making a decision about what to do with the rest of my life so that's why I took some time off from school. I sold my car and my stereo and I was all set to embark on a bohemian cross-country walking tour but I just wasn't feeling bohemian enough. Besides, there were lots of good TV shows that I didn't want to miss.

I figured that the answers would all come on their own, probably during an episode of "Days of Our Lives." If not, then fine. I'd just go back to school and take whatever came to mind. To tell you the truth, I was quite prepared to live off student loans for the rest of my pre-Viagra years.

I suppose there are a lot of other things that I could tell you about me but I just re-read the last few paragraphs and I'm already bored. So, I'll return to the grocery store...

While I was reading about some movie star's cure for flabby thighs a curious sight appeared at the checkout lane next to mine. It was a guy about my age with the brightest and ugliest red hair. The reason I mention his hair first is because it was the first thing anyone would notice about this guy. I suppose that in this enlightened age of ours we should be used to seeing red, green and blue hair around every corner but this guy's hair was so completely gaudy yet natural. It was like that fluorescent clothing that was all the rage a few years ago. It was so bright and bold and RED that if he ever went to the running of the bulls in Pamplona he would be the first to get gored.

The curious thing about him, aside from his hair, was that he was making faces at the two guys who were in front of him in line. When I say he was making faces I mean he was acting like a little kid, sticking his tongue out and screwing up his eyes and flaring his nostrils. He was jerking back and forth at the waist and swinging his little blue grocery basket into the legs of the guys in front. Grunting noises were coming out of his deformed mouth and everyone was staring gape jawed. He glanced over my way and did the oddest thing: he winked at me. Then he turned his attention back to the guys in front of him. I don't know how you feel about it, but having another guy wink at me would normally make me feel uncomfortable. The weird thing was, when he winked at me, it made me feel accepted, like he was letting me into his own personal universe. Goofy, huh? Well, I thought it was pretty out there too. As I looked at him, I realized that he reminded me of myself. For the record, we don't share the slightest physical resemblance, but for those first few seconds, it's all I could think about.

The two guys in front of him in line turned around but didn't say anything because they must have figured he was mental. Then all of a sudden the freckled face became calm and the little pig eyes narrowed, "What are you looking at?"

The two guys seemed to hold a silent debate with each other. They exchanged glances and came to the conclusion that mental or no, the red headed freak was asking for a bloody nose. They were both big guys, over six feet and carrying some two hundred pounds of muscle. One of them made his neck disappear by leaning his head back. He sneered, "Back off buddy."

Screwing himself up on his tiptoes, Red managed to bring the top of his head level with the guy's nose. Speaking directly into his foe's Adam's apple, he said, "Do you wanna take this outside?"

The guy looked like he was about to pound the little freak but his buddy had him by the arm, "Hold on Derek, you can deal with him once we're outside."

At that point everyone started to mind their own business. Eyes on shoes, wallets and purses being fidgeted around and soup can labels being read. Everyone loves to rubberneck a car accident but no one wants to be in one. It was the same thing at the store; when it seemed that there was going to be trouble in the parking lot a sort of hush fell over the checkout lanes and the only sound was the electronic beep of the price scanners.

I had my own chicken hearted nose in the Daily News and by the time I finished the by-line about a two headed man giving birth to kittens, the two guys had paid for their stuff and cast a few parting shots to the red head about seeing him outside.

Once they were out of the store I put the magazine back on the rack and looked over to see these tiny blue eyes looking at me from the next lane. I figured that the freak would start in on me next but he just stared quietly and paid the clerk without taking his eyes off me.

I turned around quickly enough and paid for my own stuff but when my groceries were bagged and held out to me by the acne potted bag boy, the red head was standing at the end of my lane waiting for me.

He was smiling and that smile seemed to transform his face into a semi-normal mask. I was set to just breeze past him but a pale, freckled hand shot out and grabbed my arm. Not roughly, more like a father keeping his son from running out into traffic.

"Hey man, can you help me out?"

That's the line that most panhandlers use and he asked it with such a beggarly tone that I thought he was referring to money. I shook my head, which is my usual polite refusal to anyone who asks me for something but he kept right on squeezing my arm and looking at me with these pleading pig eyes.

"I'm not asking for money! Those guys are going to beat the hell outta me. Can you come outside and just sorta watch my back?"

I gave him a shocked grin. The kind you give when someone is asking you for some ridiculously insane favour. I let out a guffaw on top of it, "Listen man, you were the one who started that. Don't come looking to me for help."

His eyes narrowed to a thin blue crack, "Are you chicken are something?"

"Chicken?" I laughed, "Are you mental?"

"What do you mean asking me if I'm mental? If you were going to get your butt kicked by two goons I'd help you out!"

Now the people in line were staring at us, and the only thing I wanted was to lose the freak and get the hell out of the store.

I knocked his hand off easily enough and started off, "I don't have time for this."

He was at my side, walking in a jumpy side step to keep up. His hand kept going to my sleeve to slow me down, "Zach, wait!"

I turned in a flash, "What? Do I know you?"

He sputtered, "No...why?"

"You just called me by name."

"I didn't, I said, "Man, wait."

Maybe I'd just heard wrong, but I could have sworn he had called my name. Before I could think on it further, he said, "Man, you have some kind of twisted sense of justice. You'd let a little guy like me get beat up and you won't do a thing about it!"

I paused and levelled my own steely gaze at him, "First off, you're obviously imbalanced. You started a fight with those guys and now you're asking a complete stranger to help you. That's nuts. Second..."

"Yes, second?"

"Never mind, that one point is enough. Now kindly screw off."

I started walking away again but he was on me in a flash, running in front of me and levelling a long thin finger in my face, "You're nothing but a chicken with no sense of justice!"

I didn't have to answer him. There was no point in me trying to justify myself to an obvious psychotic but that's one of my many faults. If someone thinks I'm wrong when I, and the rest of the sane world know I'm right it'll eat me up inside. If my powerful need to leave wasn't so strong at that point I would have polled the grocery store customers and proved by majority decision that I was indeed in the right. What I did instead was give him a little push back to get him out of my way.

He staggered back a couple feet and yelled out at the top of his lungs, "Now you're trying to attack me! See everyone! This bully is trying to kill me!"

I looked around wildly at the people in the checkout lanes for a show of sympathy and support but once again, only the most curious were watching and they didn't care who was right or wrong. They were only interested in the show that the red headed dork was giving.

There were a dozen different things that I could have said to him but I just shut my mouth into a grim frown and turned towards the door. I had only gone two steps when he was on me again. This time he had two hands gripping my shoulder and elbow.

"Please help me! Those guys are gonna kill me!"

I kept walking. "You should have thought of that before."

"What do you mean before? Before what? Before I was born with red hair and a pale complexion and bad teeth? Before the first gang of heartless bastards teased and tormented me?"

I wouldn't even look at him, "Those guys weren't teasing you."

"How do you know? You don't know what was going on by the meat counter! They were trying to pick up these girls and thought they could impress them by calling me names and threatening me!"

I had to slow my pace to allow the automatic door to open. I stopped right at the sensor, "You're a liar on top of being mental. Those guys didn't do anything to you because if they did you wouldn't get right behind them in line."

The door opened but I waited for his answer. He looked down at his shoes, "OK, let's say they didn't do anything. But what about the people who did? Maybe if you were tormented your whole life you'd reach the breaking point too!"

I waved my hand in dismissal and waited an extra frustrating second for the stupid automatic door to open again.

I left him behind and once I was outside I saw the two guys waiting. They did look like the type who would tease a little guy and believe me, before I grew three inches in tenth grade, I had known all about those kind of guys in an intimate way.

They had that perfect salon hair that only comes with liberal doses of hair products and a continual "running hands through hair" grooming method. Both of them were decked out in expensive clothes supporting a major running shoe company and as I walked past I caught a whiff of cologne that overpowered the exhaust fumes from the parking lot.

They were smiling on top of it all.

I had gone about twenty feet when I realised that those two were the types who would not only bully smaller guys but also go to a grocery store to pick up chicks. I think it was that realisation that made me turn around.

It didn't take long for the fight to start. Just at the moment that I turned around the red head had taken a deep breath at the door and broke into a full-fledged wailing charge. Screaming at the top of his lungs, he ran at full steam toward the bigger grocery store pick up artist. The cologned behemoth was ready for him and when the red blur banshee was within reach he let off a right hook that caught his assailant right on his tiny chin.

His head snapped back but his body kept going, colliding with the big guy's stomach and sending both of them crashing to the ground. It was a tight little tumbleweed of flailing arms and legs and I was impressed to the point of immobility. I could only stand there in amazement as the little pale fists flew without cease.

Of course a crowd gathered but nobody was doing anything. Seeing that his buddy was in trouble, big goon number two levelled two swift kicks into red's exposed ribs. That was when I joined the fray.

I leaped on top of the pile and managed to separate big dork number two. I had him in a textbook full nelson that may have looked like a prison shower room seduction but was an effective hold nonetheless. He tried to struggle out but I held him fast. In a calm voice I said, "Let 'em go at it. Keep it a fair fight." He thrashed around for a few seconds and then took a deep breath, "Ok, ok, let me go."

I decided to release the grip because I knew I couldn't hold him much longer and if I persisted he would only get madder and then I would have to contend with two hundred pounds of musky scented wrath. Besides, sometimes you have to take a chance on people's integrity and I figured he would see the justice of the situation and be calm.

As soon as he was free he spun to his left. In that same, smooth motion he cold cocked me with his elbow and my nose exploded in blinding pain. I fell backward, clutching my mushy appendage and feeling the blood flow between my fingers. I knocked my head on the pavement and heard a voice above me say, "Loser."

That's what happens when you try to do the right thing. If you don't believe me, read Confucius. "The honourable man can expect to get his butt kicked."

The next few minutes were spent in writhing agony and regret; which most of the time is the same damn thing. Once, when I was fifteen, I had the chance to score with this fantastic looking girl but I chickened out. We were at this bush party and had shared one of those huge bottles of wine with the screw on cap. The more she drank the more she got in the mood. Instead of fuelling my libido, the wine only made me somewhat nauseas and gave me a burning need to urinate. I ducked away and went into the bushes to pee and contemplate whether I was ready to leap from boy to man. I guess I took too long doing both because when I got back to her she was in the decisive arms of some Grade Ten football star. That awful memory comes back to me quite often, and when I think about what a dork I was, the regret feels the same as getting socked in the nose.

Back on the pavement, everything went black and then mellowed to grey. The noise around me seemed like background music and my own groans were alien sounds. After terrible waves of embarrassment and pain washed over me I felt a hand on my shoulder and a soft voice said, "Hey, are you alright?"
I opened my teary eyes and blinked a few times at the face that looked down at me.

It was an explosion of red leaning over me. Flaming red hair, messy and kinked, sticking out all helter skelter. Cheeks flushed and shining pink. His bloody mouth and nose, dripping in a thin line down the jaw and onto a dirty white T-shirt. Blue eyes that looked like tiny marbles floating in a bowl of tomato soup blinked and opened wide, "C'mon buddy, let me help you up."

Our two oppressors took off quickly to avoid any more trouble and the crowd thinned out and went back to their dreary lives. I took a few gasps of breath through my mouth and cringed as the freak kneeling beside me reached down and grabbed my shoulders, lifting me up and sending a fresh rush of pain to the back of my head. As soon as I was in a sitting positing he let go and clutched his chest, "Oh, my ribs are cracked!"

I held my nose, "My nose is broken!"

"I got two teeth knocked out!"

"My head is cracked open!"

"I have a rare and incurable disease!"

I let go of my nose, "What?"

His voice was completely calm, "I have a rare and incurable disease."

"You're full of it."

"Yeah, but I still have a rare and incurable disease."

"What is it?"

"You wouldn't know about it. It's rare."

"And incurable."

He nodded, "That's right."

I decided not to pursue the matter so I just stood up and offered him my hand. He took it, grimacing in pain as he straightened up, "Man, can I ask you a favour?"

"What now?"

"Can you take me to the hospital? I think I need to get my ribs looked at."

I gingerly poked the side of my nose and the sharp pain told me that it must really be broken. He added, "And you might want to get that nose checked otherwise it'll set wrong."

The thought of more time spent with a psychotic wasn't too appealing so I said, "Don't worry about my nose. And since you're dying anyway, you shouldn't bother about a few cracked ribs."

He shook his head, "Man, you're one cruel S.O.B."

I shrugged, "Maybe, but I think I did you one favour enough. See ya around."

I picked up my bag of groceries and turned to go but he was beside me once again, "Oh hey, I didn't even thank you."

I stopped and looked at him expectantly and he smiled, "Thanks!"

"You're welcome and good-bye."

"Hey, listen man. If you take me to the hospital I'll reward you."

I smirked, "A good deed is its own reward."

"Yes! I knew you had a noble side! But I'm serious here. I'll pay you."

I looked off toward the chain link fence that separated the store parking lot from the apartment complex where I lived. "Nah, it's ok. Besides, I don't even have a car."

"We'll take mine!" He dug his hand into his jean pocket and took out a set of keys. He dangled them in his hand. "You drive."

He took hold of my sleeve and started pulling me back like a kid wanting another ride on the merry-go-round. I kept shaking my head like a firm parent but he looked so pathetic and sad that I almost wavered. Then he pointed to the edge of the parking lot. His long thin finger stopped at a gleaming black Mercedes convertible, "That's my car!"

I stared like a goon at the gorgeous German engineered babe catcher and knew that even a pathological liar wouldn't bother fibbing about owning that. I stared hard at him, "Is that really your car?"

He nodded, a proud smile showing that he had indeed lost two teeth, "Yup, pretty fine isn't it?"

"Did you steal it?"

He guffawed, "I have the keys right here!" Dangling them an inch away from my fractured appendage.

Driving that car would be a dream come true but I still hesitated, pondering whether it was worth spending more close confined time with my odious companion.   Seeing my apprehension he went back to his pocket and brought out a thick roll of bills. "I'll pay you!"

My eyes bugged out at the sight of that wad but I played it cool and sighed, "Ok, let's go."

Now I suppose you think I'm some kind of creep for helping out that poor sod only because I could drive some hot car and walk away with some cash. You're probably thinking about how I only helped him out in the first place because I thought those two big guys were symbols of oppression out of my pre-pubescent past and I never even cared about whether the little guy got the snot beat out of him or not. You may be right but what would you have done? You might have just walked away, figuring that it was none of your business and then gone home and told your friends about some weird red headed goof who acted like a dork in the middle of the grocery store. Then again, maybe you would have done the right thing. Who can say? Stuff like that has to happen to us personally before we can know for sure. Even then, do we always understand our motivation for doing the right or the wrong thing?

See what I mean about how I always have to justify myself? Sorry for the interruption.

He handed me the car keys and as we walked over to the car I was simply enthralled with how good it looked the closer we got. Sure enough, the keys slid into the lock smoothly and the door flew open with an inviting swoosh. We put our groceries in the back and I forgot all about the pain north of my neck once my denim met the moulded leather seat. Even though my knees were jammed under the steering wheel from the seat being positioned so close I had never felt more comfortable in my life.

I put the key in the ignition and found the button that glided the seat back, down, and around into a perfect position. There was a little whirring sound as the lumbar support was adjusted with a skill surpassing the hands of the most gifted Swedish masseuse.

My eyes swept over the instrumentation and with an ecstatic little gasp, I started the engine, feeling the engine rumble like a lion's purr. Gentle wisps of conditioned air caressed me as my hands firmly grasped the steering wheel, ready to end the foreplay.

Like an alarm clock on Monday morning, a shrill voice broke the spell of my dream. "Can you hurry it up? I'm having some trouble breathing."

I sputtered, "Sorry. I've never even been in a Mercedes."

"Same as any other car, let's go."

I shifted into reverse and slowly backed out of the stall. I took a deep breath when I put it in first and cautiously cruised past the drab domestic cars that were parked on either side. The Fords and Chevys were soldiers with upraised swords, honouring passing royalty as I glided past with my chin raised to keep my crown level.

"C'mon man, punch it. Medical emergency."

The car even seemed to be getting impatient rumbling along in first but I waited until I was out of the parking lot until I dropped it into second and roared away in the opposite direction of my apartment.

"That's the spirit. Don't stop till we're in the emergency ward."

Once the car was going a fluid fifty miles an hour I felt his eyes on me once again. I glanced over and he had a beaming smile, which looked pretty gruesome what with the blood and the missing teeth.

He offered his hand, "Andy Tiernan."

I took my hand off the leather wrapped shifter and shook his hand, "Zachary Kinfleisich."

He grinned, "King Flea Itch."

I turned back to the road, pushing the car into the far lane and passing a green van. In a dry voice I said, "You're Funny."

"You've heard that one before."

It didn't sound like a question but I answered anyway. "About a million times before I even hit the third grade."

He looked back to the road, "I didn't think seven year olds were that witty."

"You'd be amazed."

"Well, do you mind if I call you Zack?"

I shrugged, "Most people do."

He smiled, "In that case I'll call you Zachary."

I parked the car on the east side of the Misericordia Hospital. It was located on the west end of town and it was called, naturally, Misery-cordia. It was probably the same seven year olds who came up with the name.

Andy and I walked through the big automatic sliding doors and went straight to the emergency desk. I had to support Andy as he winced and staggered with each step he took. He didn't say anything and I have to admit, I was starting to not mind him as much since he began to act like a normal guy with cracked ribs.

We leaned against the counter and filled out our forms before taking our seats next to a guy with a bloody rag wrapped around his hand. We didn't say much as we looked around the waiting room, checking out the fidgety agonies that sat around us.

There was the bloody hand guy; a woman who kept making exaggerated retching noises, and a teenager clutching his arm. There was a mother with what seemed like fourteen kids, and they were all running around and being pests. They were kicking the walls, banging on the coffee vending machine and yelping to their mother who looked like she wanted to shotgun the entire clan.

After fifteen minutes, the guy with the bloody hand, who at that point was in tears, was led inside by a very tired looking nurse. Within ten minutes, an ambulance had come screeching into the parking lot and two paramedics rushed in, wheeling a stretcher laden with a fat biker plugged full of tubes and other life saving instruments.

Andy squirmed in his seat but said nothing. He just stared at the growing number of people who came in and took their seats: three young guys with various wounds, another woman with two kids in tow and an old man who kept coughing up buckets of phlegm.

Andy leaned closer to me, "What time is it?"
I checked my watch, "Almost eleven."
"How long have we been here?"
"About an hour."
He nodded resolutely. "I'm not waiting anymore."

He stood up and hobbled over to the reception desk and I turned to watch him try to reason with the no-nonsense nurse who simply shook her head and motioned for him to return to his seat.

Andy came back and sat down heavily, letting out a sigh. "How's your nose?"
"Hurts. How are the ribs?"
"Killin' me."
I tried a smile. "Keep it in perspective. After all, you've got a terminal disease, what's a few cracked ribs."
"Yeah, but I wasn't planning on dying today."

We didn't say anything for another few minutes. Andy sat bolt upright, staring straight ahead. Minutes crawled on and he didn't even blink. I thought that he looked like a pot about to boil over and I was right. All of a sudden he took a huge breath and let out a blood-curdling scream.

His hands gripped the sides of the chair as he threw his head back and howled like a lunatic. It was a high-pitched, woman-in-a-horror-movie scream that made everyone in the room jump. It lasted for a full twenty seconds and then after another deep breath he started again.

An intern appeared out of nowhere pushing a litter. Andy kept screaming and when the intern tried to calm him down he jumped to his feet and leapt right onto the stretcher, still screaming. There was nothing for the intern to do but push him off toward an examination room.

The scream trailed off and eventually died, leaving all the patients-in-waiting heaving sighs of relief before returning to their own personal misery.

Another half hour passed before I was called in. The nurse led me to a tiny room down a long hallway. I was informed that a doctor would be right with me and after another half an hour of staring at the cotton balls I was ready to let out my own howling scream.

The pain in my nose was more annoying than anything as the blood pulsed rhythmically, sending the occasional drop onto my lap. I lay down on the paper covered examination table and feeling completely bagged, promptly fell asleep. I was woken shortly after by a young doctor who looked more tired and irritated than I was. He poked my nose a few times and wiggled it around in between his palms and then told me it wasn't even broken and I should just ice it when I get home.

Doctors just don't give a damn anymore. It's not like when Marcus Welby was the industry standard. Don't get me wrong; those doctors on ER are pretty good too. The friendly doctor on Little House on the Prairie was great too. I think the problem with me is that I watch too much TV. Reality can never match up to fine quality programming.

I went back into the reception area and saw that the only person there was Andy and he was obviously waiting for me. He was stretched out with his feet up on another chair; his eyes were closed and his arms were folded across his chest. I looked down at him for a moment and thought to myself that he looked kind of peaceful and innocent. After that millisecond was over I shook the car keys under his nose.

His eyes shot open and his legs jerked off the chair, making him wince and grab his sore ribs. He looked around wildly before he noticed me. He smiled, "Hey man, are we ready to go?"

I shrugged, "I dunno about "we", but I'm going home."

He stood up, "Man, can I ask you a favour?"

"How many times are you going to ask me that?

He grinned, "I'm pretty doped up and the doctor says I can't drive."

"Well can't you call someone to pick you up?"

"C'mon man, then I'll have to leave my car here. Help me out, be a pal."

I levelled my eyes at him, "I'm not your pal. I'm a complete stranger who somehow ended up with a broken nose and three hours of my life wasted."

He stared at my nose, "It isn't broken."

I threw my arms up in desperation, "That isn't the point!"

He turned his head slightly to the side, "What is the point?"

I put the keys in his palm, "The point is that I'm going home."

"But what about your reward?"

I held out my hand, "OK, pay me then."

His puppy dog eyes went into overdrive, "Please! Please! Give me a ride home!"

I looked over my shoulder and saw the nurse was giving me the dirtiest look that she could muster. I turned away from Broom Hilda and said in a lowered voice, "C'mon man, I just want to go home and get to bed."

He sank down to his knees and his voice went up a notch, "Please! I'm begging you not to leave me stranded here!"

I growled, "Ok, get up you worm! I'll drive you home!"

He jumped up, wincing at the pain once again, "You really are a pal!"

I started for the door, "No, I'm just a sucker for an ugly face."

He didn't say a word to me as we walked to the car and once I was back in that LazyBoy on wheels I felt comfortable enough to drop off to sleep. Andy gave me directions to his house and I moaned when I heard that it was all the way across town.

I turned to him angrily, "What the hell are you doing shopping on the west end when you live on the south side?"

He gave me a huge grin and reached back into his grocery bag. He pulled out a yellow box of chocolate covered raisins, "These!" He said triumphantly. "The best chocolate covered raisins in the city!" He tore open the box and poured out a handful, "Want some?"

I shook my head and he held his chocolaty hand out to me, "It's ok, take some. I bought twelve boxes!"

I shook my head disgustedly and drove off, while he munched his chocolates in supreme glee.

As he ate he hummed some upbeat song, nodding his head from side to side like some demented maestro. In between mouthfuls he looked out the window and made little comments like, "Hey, lookit that weirdo!" and "Pass this guy, I want to see his nose! It was huge!"

After about ten minutes of his bouncing up and down, pointing, gesticulating and humming I sneered, "You don't act like you're doped up. You could have driven home yourself."

He turned back to me and slumped down in his seat. He let out a melodramatic yawn and slurred, "I'm so tired. I can't wait to get home."

I made three wrong turns because of Andy's skewered directions and when we finally drove up to a huge Victorian house I was ready to pass out from fatigue. I couldn't make out much of the house in the dark but judging from the ritzy neighbourhood we were in I knew it had to be a reasonable facsimile of a mansion. I said, "Is this your parent's house?"

He shook his head, "No, it's mine."

I looked at him incredulously, "You're so full of it."

He shrugged and pointed to the black gates that barred the driveway, "Go up there."

I pulled over next to this control panel and Andy said, "The code is 5874."

I wondered why he would trust me with the code, after all, for all he knew, I was a psychopathic axe murderer and before my finger even reached the 5 he let out a chuckle, "I trust you, Zachary, my life is now in your hands. Even if you are a psychopathic axe murderer."

My body gave a little shiver and then I punched in the code and the wrought iron gates swung open. I slowly drove up, trying to peer through the dense hedges that lined the driveway but all was black and my vision was starting to blur. I stopped in front of the triple car garage and shut the car off, "Well, this is it."

He smiled, "It sure is."

After a brief pause I said, "I don't suppose you'd be so kind as to call me a cab."

He shook his head, "Not a chance, you're my guest tonight."

"No way. Not a chance. I'm going home. In fact, if I'm not in my own bed in one hour I'm going to kill you. I mean really kill you. Genuine homicide."

He kept smiling, "Oh no, I insist."

I was about to make good on my threat when all of a sudden a light came on from inside and the front door opened. A tall figure, obviously female, came running out toward the car. Andy opened his door and slowly got out to greet the woman, "That's my sister, Cynthia. She's gonna freak out at me."

Now, let me say this: I may have been dead tired and groggy to beat hell but this woman was the most gorgeous creature I had ever laid eyes on. Tall, blonde, and in my mind, built like a brick wet dream. I got out of the car and stared at her in abject worship.

Andy came around beside me and as we watched her approach he said, "Why do people say that a good looking woman is built like something made of brick? I for one have never been aroused by masonry."

I was about to express a great deal of shock at having my thoughts invaded by an amateur psychic but Cynthia was already upon us.

Andy said to the vision, "This is Zachary. I'm trying to talk him into staying the night."

He turned back to me, "Zachary, are you sure you won't change your mind?"

I smiled at Cynthia, "OK, I'll stay."

Day Two

Monday the Eleventh

It would be nice to say that Cynthia was immediately swept away by my charm and grace but after our introduction she didn't give me a second glace. In defence of my ego, it might have been because once she saw Andy's cuts and bruises she turned into a sisterly Florence Nightingale, fussing and fretting over his ailments with a nurturing dementia.

I followed at a distance as she dragged the poor little guy into a bathroom and began to wash and swathe every nick on him. Andy didn't protest but he stood there with a surly look on his face, avoiding my gaze out of embarrassment. She questioned him mercilessly about what had happened but the only answers she got were shrugs and mumbled sentence fragments.

When she finished, she clutched his chin in her palm and levelled firm eyes into his, "You can explain everything tomorrow." Then she dropped the washcloth into the clothes hamper and disappeared down the hall. I figured she was off whipping up a pot of chicken soup for her little brother but I never found out as Andy sullenly led me to a guest room on the third floor and folded down the bed for me.

After he fluffed up the pillows his smile slowly came back, "Thanks for staying. I'll make you a big breakfast in the morning."
I looked back toward the hallway, "So that's your sister."
He punched the pillow down onto the bed, "Yeah, she drives me nuts sometimes but she's ok."

I nodded, "She seems really nice."

Of course when I said that she seemed nice what I really meant was that I wanted to do despicably sordid sexual acrobatics with her. Andy seemed to know it too and he looked back to me with a hard look that lasted long enough to know that I had offended him. It's natural for a brother to be protective of his sister and after seeing how Cynthia fretted over him, it was obvious that they shared a close relationship.

It isn't like that with me, as both of my sisters are complete cows and I would set them up with any number of bikers just for the fun of it.

Andy looked like he was going to admonish me and I was even set to apologise but suddenly his expression changed. He said a cheerful good night and left the room before I could say anything.

I undressed and got into bed. Like the seats in the Mercedes, the bed was extremely comfortable and I fell asleep in minutes. As you can see, I'm not one of those people who need to take stock of their surroundings in order to get comfortable enough to fall asleep. My parents moved every couple years and since I turned eighteen I've had seven different apartments. Strange noises, bumps in the night and creaky old houses don't bother me a bit. It must be the gypsy in me.

About seven hours later the sun poured through white lace curtains and I stretched, yawned and regretfully got out of bed. I opened the door and peeked out into the hall but not a red head or blonde was stirring. I stepped onto the plush carpeting and softly walked down one end until I found the bathroom. I splashed some water on my face, noticing that there were two dark bags under my eyes. I stuck my tongue out at my reflection for no sane reason whatsoever and then answered nature's call.

Back in the hall I listened for any noise but aside from the toilet's watery hum, the house was dead silent. I went back to the room and put my clothes on and then headed for the stairs.

After a quick inspection, I found that the second floor was also deserted but when I was halfway down the second flight of stairs I heard the TV on a few rooms over. I went down a hall, through the kitchen and traced the sound to a sunken family room. I could see the back of Andy's head as he sat on the couch, facing a huge TV that must have cost more than my student loan.

He was watching The Flintstones and chuckling to himself as Fred told Wilma some story about why he and Barney were out all night. I cleared my throat and Andy jumped, turning in his seat and pointing the remote at me like it was a ray gun. The look of surprise on his face contorted into a huge grin, "Zachary! I was wondering when you'd wake up! How did you sleep?"

"Good thanks. How are the ribs?"

He gave his chest a mild poke with his index finger, "Good as new."

I nodded slowly, pretending to look around the room while I thought of something to say. Andy kept grinning and after what seemed like a one-sided awkward silence I shrugged, "So... are you going to give me a ride home or should I call a cab?"

He jumped to his feet, "No! I promised you breakfast and I never break a promise!"

I looked around the room again and thought to myself that I didn't really want to stay.

"Don't go! Please!" Andy added with just the right dose of desperation.

I was kind of hungry and at that point, I also didn't have any plans for the day aside from beginning my vacation by watching a few cartoons of my own, so I shrugged, "Ok."

As impossible as it seemed, Andy's grin grew even wider as he bounded off toward the kitchen, "Come on!"

I stuck my hands in my pockets and shuffled off after him.

By the time I got to the kitchen he was already tying an apron around his waist and noisily pulling out frying pans and other gastronomic implements. I sat down at one of the kitchen chairs facing the stove and pulled out my pack of cigarettes. "Is it alright if I smoke?"

His eyes lit up as he practically leapt over to one of the cupboards and pulled out a huge glass ashtray. He placed it in front of me and just as I was about to light a cigarette he practically screamed, "Wait! Have one of mine!"

With another energetic bounce he was at what I presumed to be the junk drawer. He tore it open, making the contents clunk and clink together. He took out a strange looking blue cigarette pack and flipped it open, "These are from Turkey! Impossible to get here!"

I put my own cigarette back in my pack and gingerly took out a long, thin stick with a white filter. He flicked open my Zippo and lit it for me, waiting for my expression as I took a drag.

It tasted all right and since he was so enthusiastic about the whole thing I gave him a smile and said, "It's good."

He beamed. "Damn right it's good! You can't get them here!"

I'm going to pause here and say that I've since kicked the smoking habit. Many people start because they figure that smoking makes them look cool. I suppose that theory would work if every guy on the planet looked like James Dean and every woman like… well, like some hot looking movie star who smoked. But the fact is most people look like idiots when they smoke and yellow teeth don't look cool on anyone, even hot looking movie stars. It took me eight attempts at quitting to finally stop and I was so grumpy and miserable and I coughed up like fifteen gallons of brown sludge from my lungs. Pretty cool huh? So don't smoke. There, my public service address is over. Let's go back to the kitchen.

After another smiling silence Andy turned back to the cupboards and pulled out one of those floppy chef hats and put it on. He grabbed a spatula out of another drawer and then turned back to me, striking a culinary pose, "Isn't this hat the coolest?"

I gave him a bouncy nod full of sarcasm, "Wicked."

The smile melted off his face and the corners of his mouth dropped as he tore the chef's hat off and flung it across the room. It landed on top of the refrigerator and we both looked at it at for a second or two. I don't know why but that hat seemed like a metaphor for some intangible childhood ideal. His taking it off just because of my sarcastic reply made me feel guilty but as soon as Andy smiled again, I felt forgiven.

He said, "I'm sorry, I should have asked but do you have time for breakfast?"

I took another drag off the cigarette, "Sure."

"You don't have to go to work or anything?"

"Nah, this is my vacation."

"You go to school?"

"Yeah, at the University."

He seemed really interested as his eyes grew a little wider, "Oh? What are you taking?"

I smiled, "My sweet time deciding what to major in."

He smiled back, "Well, you're young yet. There's lots of time for you to decide."

I shrugged, "I guess."

He gave me this piercing look like he was taking Polaroids of my soul. I turned away and when I glanced back to him, he had already gone over to the fridge and began taking out the eggs and an armful of plastic wrapped packages. "Bacon, eggs, sausages. That sound alright to you?"

My stomach growled on cue, "Sounds great."

He went to the counter and began unwrapping the packages and taking out plates and forks. I looked around the kitchen, taking note of the fancy stainless steel oven, the huge, matching fridge with icemaker and other yuppie belongings. "Last night you said that this was your house."

He nodded, his back still to me, "That's right."

"Seems like a pretty nice place for a twenty year old to own."

"I'm twenty five."

"Are you a drug dealer or something?"

He laughed, "Of course, don't I look like a dangerous gangster?"

"So, is this your parent's place?"

He continued moving the pots and plates and food around, "No, they're dead. How do you want your eggs?"

He said it so bluntly that it made the hairs on the back of my neck stand up. "I'm sorry."

"I said how do you want your eggs."

"No, I heard you. I meant I was sorry about your parents."

He turned to me with a hard look as he leaned back against the counter, "Were you the one who broke in here and shot them while they were in bed?"

My answer was a shocked look as I shook my head. He quickly turned around again, "Then you don't have anything to be sorry about. Now how do you want your eggs?"

"Um..."

He turned his head to me, displaying another broad grin. "Scrambled right?"

I nodded.

"Bo-ring!"

Whether it was boring or not, he got out a bowl and began to break the eggs and whisk them with a fork. He put the frying pan on the stove and turned the heat up, putting a huge dollop of butter in with the other hand.

He pointed to the half full coffee pot, "Want some coffee?"
"Sure."

He grabbed a cup and filled it, "Black, right?"

I nodded and said, "Yeah, black." In a voice that was half joking and half freaked out, I said, "You must be psychic."

"Yeah," he said with a laugh, "I made my fortunes as a breakfast psychic, going from town to town, guessing how people take their eggs and coffee." He laughed again at his own joke and said, "Actually, I just kinda figured it out. Y'know, no nonsense, no frills, take the bull by the horns, black coffee and scrambled eggs kind of guy."

I chuckled, "Yeah, that and the fact that I'm lactose intolerant."

He handed me the cup and looked at me with an ultra sincere smile, "Thank you for telling me that Zachary; I'm glad you feel you can trust me with something that personal."

I took the cup from him and wrinkled my eyebrows, "Uh, no problem."

He went back to his labours and after I took a sip of coffee I said casually, "So it's just you and your sister?"

"Yup, that's right."

"You two must be pretty close."

"I suppose."

"Is she at work?"

"Sort of. She volunteers at the hospital."

"She doesn't mind you having strangers over for breakfast?"

He left the bacon and sausages sizzle as he turned to me once again. "You like her huh?"

I answered quickly and defensively, "I was just asking a question."

He waved his hand, "its ok. Most guys do. They take one look at her and swear to do great deeds of daring-do just for a smile." He looked out the window wistfully, "She never gives any of them the time of day." He looked back to me with a smile, "I think she's in training for the nunnery."

I smiled back, but inside my foolish ego told me that I might just be the one to change all that.

His pale blue eyes grew suddenly sharp, "But who knows? Maybe you'll change all that. You might be the one to tame the Shrew."

Once again my neck tingled as it felt like he was reading my mind. Nevertheless, I let out a nervous laugh, "Why do you say that? Does your sister go for the no nonsense black coffee drinker types?"

He laughed back, "Don't forget the sensible scrambled eggs!"

It was obvious that he wasn't going to say anymore on the subject of his sister because he turned back to the stove and started telling me his personal views on cholesterol as he flipped half a pound of bacon into the frying pan.

By the time I had finished my cigarette I learned that he thought most physical ailments were caused by fluoride in the drinking water or gamma rays from the planet Pluto. OK, to be honest, I really wasn't listening. I was still thinking about Cynthia.

The only thing I added to the conversation was a few grunts and a few sarcastic replies. He didn't seem to mind though, as he continued lambasting the medical profession and water treatment plants. After a pause of maybe three seconds he switched gears again, "Hey, do you have a cell phone?"

I shook my head.

"Good, they cause brain tumours."

I nodded.

"Why don't you have a cell phone?" He asked.

Because I didn't have anyone to call and nobody called me. I only shrugged in response but once again, he seemed to squint at me as if reading my mind.

"I'm sorry." He said softly.

"About what?" I barked.

"Nothing." He said in that same soft, sympathetic tone. I decided not to pursue the matter, not wanting to have a hideous looking little geek felling sorry for me.

My stomach was starting to seriously growl by the time he was finished cooking and when he set the plate down in front of me I practically inhaled all the eggs and half the bacon. He poured himself a cup of coffee and sat down at the table, sipping slowly and smiling at me. His constant staring was a little unnerving but when I finished the breakfast and lit a cigarette, I was too satisfied to let it bother me.

He poured me another cup of coffee and cleared the plate away; he took a cigarette out of the pack, lighting it with a couple small coughs. After another awkward silence I smiled, "Thanks a lot man, that was really good."

He lifted his coffee cup in a salute, "My pleasure."

More silence.

"Well, I hate to eat and run but..."

He looked at me shrewdly, "I thought you didn't have any plans. Why do you have to rush off?"

I shifted uneasily, "I don't have any plans but I should be getting home anyway."

"But why? What can you do at home that you can't do here?"

"Nothing I guess but still..."

"Still nothing! You can have a shower here! You can watch TV! C'mon Zachary, we can hang out, have some fun!"

I stood up, "Listen Andy, I appreciate the bed and breakfast but look..." I paused and tried a smile, "I've only known you about twelve hours. I hate to be so blunt but I don't really need another friend."

I didn't want to offend him but I needn't have worried about that, as all he did was stare at me for a second before he smiled, "Don't you?"

"Don't I what?"

"Need a friend."

My voice raised involuntarily, "What?"

He lifted his hands in a placating manner, "I may just be shooting in the dark here but you seem like a loner."

I scoffed, "You're just chock full of little observations aren't you?" I let out a laugh, "I've got lots of friends!"

Of course he was right. I didn't have any friends. That sounds really pathetic but don't go feeling sorry for me. It isn't like I'm this bookworm geek who nobody talks to. I hang out with some guys from school that I go to the bars and parties with. I suppose they're all right in their own way but I wouldn't consider them friends. Most of them are shoplifters and car thieves and I wouldn't tell any of them anything personal if my life depended on it. The thing is, people generally annoy me and Andy was doing a good job of that too.

He motioned to the chair, "I'm sorry, I was out of line. Please, sit down."

I didn't want to sit down, "Look man, let me call a cab and then we can shake hands and go live our own lives."

His head drooped and he sighed, "I'll give you a ride home."

"That's ok. A cab will be fine."

His voice rose to an irritating pitch, "Please, let me drive you home."

I let out a sigh of my own, "Fine, whatever."

He stood up and patted his pockets, "Oh, is it ok if I take you on a little detour first?"

I groaned, "Where?"

His head snapped up and his eyes were glazed over, "California."

"Ha, ha."

"I'm serious!"

I turned around, "Where's the phone? I'm calling a cab."

"Don't tell me you would turn down an all expense paid trip to the coast?"

I saw the phone on a small table in the corner of the kitchen and headed toward it, "OK, I won't tell you."

I picked up the phone and dialled 411. Andy came over to my side and whispered, "I'll give you a hundred thousand dollars."

I laughed, "Yeah right."

The operator came on the line and I asked her for the cab company's number. Andy slammed his finger down on the button, "I said I'll give you a hundred thousand dollars to go to California!"

I dialled the number again without even looking at him, "I heard you."

He hit the button again, this time keeping his hand over the cradle, "Zachary, sit down. Please!"

I kept the receiver in my hand, "Just shut up. I've had enough."

He grabbed my sleeve and began to pull me over to the table, "I'm dead serious! I'll pay you and I'll get my bankbook to prove that I have the money. I'll cut you a cheque right now!"

I shook my head, "This isn't about money. Don't you see how insane you're acting? Let me go home."

He was starting to cry as he pulled at my sleeve. His voice was harsh and low, "Please sit down and let me explain. Please just hear me out and then if you really want to go home then I won't stop you. I swear."

I put the receiver down in its cradle and went over to the table. I tried to sound gentle but I could never do a good job of that. "OK, explain."

He sat down, wiping his runny nose on his sleeve. He took out another cigarette and lit it, letting out the same little coughs as he inhaled. After a couple drags he looked at me with red tinged eyes, "I'm going to die. I told you that yesterday and you didn't believe me but it's true. I don't know how much time I have left. If the doctors were right, I should have been dead a month ago."

I leaned forward, "What is this disease then? What's it called?"

He glared at me. "Don't interrupt." He took a long drag and coughed out a bluish cloud of smoke, "I found out I was going to die about six months ago. I didn't believe it at first and I went to about ten different doctors but they all said the same thing. My time was up. The only thing they differed on was how long I had. Some said a month, two months; a grand optimist said six months. A few of them gave me a special diet to follow and another sent me to a homeopathic doctor who covered me in leaves and put a tuning fork over my groin." He grinned, "But no amount of Vedic chants was going to do it. There was absolutely nothing I could do and I didn't leave the house for a month. I was depressed and sick from not eating or sleeping. Saturday was the first day in six months that I actually smiled. I decided that if I'm going to go, I'd go happy. I'll go with a bang." He inhaled deeply on his cigarette and butted it out, "I only started smoking yesterday!" We both smiled.

"So this is it, my first and last hurrah. I've got the means to do something special before I die but I really need you to help me. I just want to have some fun, make my mark in life, and do something special so it won't be as if I never existed." He looked down at the ashtray. "I want to see the ocean before I die."

I looked away from him and closed my eyes, which is something I always do whenever I have to make an important decision. I took a deep breath and thought what the hell.

Andy jumped to his feet and gave me a hug, pinning my arms against my sides. "Yes! I knew you'd do it!"

His intuitiveness was getting kind of freaky. I mean, I didn't even raise an eyebrow when I changed my mind but he just knew. I tell you, that kind of thing really freaks me out.

He let go after a final squeeze and then took a step back, looking at me with a delirious grin, "And you don't have to pack. When I said all expense paid, I meant it. Total RFB! Room, food, beverage and yes, clothes! Souvenirs! Cigarettes! Change for pay toilets! Everything!" He took out the car keys and thrust them at me in a shaking fist, "You drive the first leg and then we'll switch when you get tired!" Suddenly he drew the keys back, "Wait! We can't leave just yet!" He turned around and started pacing the floor, "We have to make some plans! Road maps, munchies! What CDs should we take?" He looked back to me, "You have to shower! I'll take care of everything! This is great! It'll be just like in the movies!"

I hated to end his excitement but I said, "Andy, why the hell don't we just fly?"

He pointed his finger at me, "That's exactly what they say in the movies too!"

"I haven't been to the movies in a while. What's the usual response?"

"Why, that getting there is half the fun! The journey is almost as important because we'll have time to talk and get to know one another." I cringed but he continued, "See the country! Maybe meet some interesting people! They never fly in the movies! The terminally ill guy always insists on driving!" He paused, trying to think of another reason, "It's spiritual!"

He went back to the table and lit another cigarette and took a long drag and it seemed to calm him down a bit. "I'll go get the supplies. You can relax here, have a shower and watch some TV. I won't be long." He started for the door and then paused, "What size pants do you wear?"
"Why?"
"I'm going to buy you clothes!"
"I'll buy my own clothes."
He looked me up and down, which made it apparent that he was going to buy me clothes whether I liked it or not. He cast a final glance at my legs and then waved, going out the door. I leaned forward and yelled, "Don't buy me any clothes!"

Once he was gone the house was eerily quiet and I got up, stretched and wondered what kind of mess I had got myself into. I was in a state of disbelief and didn't really think that we were actually going to go to California. Andy seemed like such a little kid that everything he did seemed like a game; going for a cross country drive was make believe and nothing more.

Of course, I reasoned, Andy also seemed like a guy who would just tramp off at the spur of the moment. It was also apparent that he had the means to do it, including the hundred thousand dollar companionship fee.

I went over to the stove and poured myself another cup of coffee when I heard Andy's car pull away. "This is really going to happen." I said to myself and then daydreamed of LA starlets and white beaches. "Who knows, it might end up being a lot of fun." After I said that I knew that I was talking to myself far too much so I wandered around the main floor, being a snoop.

Most people will snoop around when they're in a strange bathroom. That's human nature and if I'm to be left in an empty house then as far as I'm concerned the whole place is just one big medicine cabinet. I know that's rude and inappropriate but you can blame my parents for my behaviour. If my mother would have spent less time worrying about whether my underwear were ironed she would have had more time to teach me about not snooping around. My dad worked at the office for ten hours a day before he took off for good and the only lessons he brought home were to never go into the insurance business. He could have also added to never screw around with your secretary if she has a jealous professional wrestler for a boyfriend. But that's another story.

The point is I figure that I can get away with blaming my parents for everything. Basically, accountability sucks.

You'd think that a big luxurious house would be a snooper's dream but this place was so clean and orderly that after poking my nose in two rooms I got bored. The most interesting thing in the whole damn place was the TV, which had a "picture in picture" function so I could watch two different soap operas at the same time.

After that I watched a game show and a program on PBS about hyenas. Then some talk show came on about pantsuit wearing single mother lesbians and then I began to get really bored. Even cable TV has its limitations.

Andy still hadn't returned and the afternoon was wearing away. I held a debate with myself during the commercials whether I should leave but the thought of a hundred thousand dollars and Andy's pleading little eyes kept me there. Besides, I had told him I would go with him on his spiritual journey and if there's one thing I can't stand, it's people who say they are going to do something and then don't.

My parents helped instil that in me by being the worst examples of keeping their word. I bet my father promised to take me to the zoo about five hundred times when I was kid and the only time I ever saw a real live spider monkey was when I was sixteen. Tom Macgee, my only real friend in junior high school, cut class with me and we spent the day at the zoo, eating popcorn and watching Lucy the Elephant defecate.

I kept channel surfing until some lame after school special came on. I think it was the classic, "The Boy Who Had Nits", starring Scott Baio. I'm just kidding, I don't know what it was called, but it made me daydream about how much I wanted to be like Scott Baio when he was a cool teenage heartthrob in "Happy Days." I was pretty much a loser when I was a kid. I grabbed a box of low fat crackers from the kitchen and munched away, brushing the crumbs off my chest into the thick carpet.

About ten minutes later I finally heard a car drive up and then the door opened. Keys were dropped on a table, shoes were kicked off and soft footsteps came into the room.

It was Cynthia, standing in the glorious sunlight and wearing a scowl that contrasted deeply to her hospital candy striper uniform.

"Hi!" I mumbled, causing tiny bits of cracker crumbs to fly out of my mouth.

She was obviously impervious to any kind of charm, "Where's Andy?"

I quickly swallowed, set the box of crackers down on the coffee table and stood up, "He went out to get some stuff, he said he would be back right away."

"And when was that?"

I looked down at my watch, "About three hours ago."

She looked away with a frown, "Typical."

I was going to tell her Andy's plan of going off to California but it would have been way too awkward. She would find out soon enough from her brother and I didn't want to have to sit there and explain the strange conversation that he and I had that morning.

She marched over to the table and snatched up the box of crackers, "Feeling right at home aren't you?" Without giving me a chance to answer she stormed off to the kitchen.

I could feel blood starting to rush into my cheeks as my mind went blank. She was so damn good looking that I was left completely dazed. Also, when dealing with a woman who is apparently mad at the world and everyone in it, the best thing to do is just sit down and shut up. So that's what I did.

I could hear her collecting the dirty dishes in the kitchen and I regretted not washing up. Then cupboards were opened and their contents loudly moved around. I imagined that she was checking to see if I scoffed any caviar or imported Swiss sugar cookies, which naturally, I had.

She spent the next half hour in the kitchen and I stayed where I was, watching TV and cringing with every loud noise that came from the next room. I could feel myself getting closer to the mother of all anxiety attacks with each passing second so I began to switch through the channels in a furious pace, letting my subconscious absorb the video bits that flew by.

Just when I was ready to bolt, a car drove up and I waited on the edge of my seat for Andy to come in. Cynthia came out of the kitchen and walked past me to the entrance, keeping her eyes zeroed in on the door.

Andy came in carrying an armload of packages and the smile that was on his face dropped along with his burdens as soon as he saw his sister.

She didn't waste a second, "Where have you been?"
"Out." He mumbled as he rearranged the packages on the floor.
"What's all this?"
He gave another incomprehensible mumble.
"I said what is this stuff?"
"It's supplies." Andy said without looking up.
"Supplies for what?"
"For a trip."
Before she could grill him further he was out the door but she leaped over the bags after him.

I could hear her asking him questions but no replies could be made out. A minute later he was back in the house, carrying another armful of bags. He simply dropped them on the floor and went back out, almost running into Cynthia, who was right at his heels. When he came back for the third time, the tension between the two of them was stifling. Andy even seemed to be holding up with a menacing scowl equal to hers.

He took off his shoes and came into the room with a stern look, "Hey Zachary, sorry it took me so long but I had a lot of stuff to get."

I only shrugged and Cynthia barged in, her voice sounding like a bucket of rusty nails and broken glass. "Andrew Tiernan you answer me right now!"

Andy spun around and faced her, "You aren't my mother! So just shut up!"

Cynthia's jaw dropped for a second and then her scowl returned this time levelled at me, like I was the one to blame for his impertinence.

Andy turned back, "You didn't shower."

I stuttered, "I was watching TV..."

"And eating my food!" Cynthia bellowed.

Andy looked straight ahead, "Cynthia, I told you to shut up." His eyes came back to me, "You better go shower, we're leaving right away."

"Where do you think you're going?" The witch asked.

He ignored her, "There's no way I'm gonna be in the same car with you if you don't shower." Then he grinned, "I'm kinda particular about personal hygiene."

She growled, "I asked you a question Andy."

He kept right on ignoring her, walking back to the entrance and picking up two bags and bringing them back to me, "Here, I got you some clothes."

I took the bags dumbly and Andy grinned, making a shooing motion with his hands, "Now go! Go on!"

I gave Cynthia my best innocent bystander look and then headed for the stairs. The two of them waited until I got to the first landing before they started in on each other again. First Cynthia's screaming barrage of questions and then Andy's short, curse-laden variations on "It's none of your business."

The distance from their argument to the third floor bathroom was sufficiently far enough for me to drown them out completely once I turned on the water. There seemed to be an inexhaustible supply of hot water so I stayed in the shower as long as possible. I hoped that when I was done the yelling and screaming would be over but even through the heavy oak door, muffled voices an octave higher than before could be heard.

I inspected the clothes that Andy had bought for me and was truly relieved when I saw that they were conservative, jeans and T-shirt type apparel. I was worried that he would have got me plaid knickerbockers and velvet turtlenecks three sizes too small. I put the new underwear on and looked in the mirror. I was pleased that he got me boxers because I hadn't worn briefs since I was twelve years old. Back then I thought that boxers were a lot cooler than briefs. Looking cool was very important to me then. You might have seen me on the corner, wearing nothing but my underwear and smoking a cigarette.

I picked out a pair of jeans and a black shirt. After I got dressed I stared at my reflection. All decked out in new clothes with a marble bathtub with gold fixtures behind me, it really hammered home just how bizarre everything had become in the past twenty hours.

I always have these comic book moments of revelation. I'll do an actual double take and then shake my head and go on. I think it's a much better way of going through life, rather than worrying and fretting about every little thing like my semi-neurotic mother would have me do.

I combed my hair and opened the door slowly, letting the steam billow out behind me. The voices became clearer with each tentative step I took and when I reached the landing I heard, "For the last time, we're going and there's no way you can stop me!"

"You don't even know that guy! How can you just take off on a trip with him?"

"His name is Zach."

"I don't care what his name is!" Cynthia screeched. "I don't like the look of him!"

"You don't like the look of anyone!"

"He could be a psycho axe murderer! He could be a junkie or a criminal!"

I thought to myself, "And you could be the creature from the bitch lagoon."

Andy let out an inexplicable snicker and then said, "He's none of those things."

She paused, as if considering, and then said, "He's probably a con man trying to steal your money!"

Andy's voice was calm and quiet, "He's not a junkie, a criminal or a con man. He's just lonely."

I felt myself grow cold then and after a long pause Cynthia said, "If you're so dead set on going, then I'm coming along."

"No freaking way!" Andy screamed.

"Andy, watch your tone with me!"

"There's no way you're coming!"

"Just like I can't stop you from going, you can't stop me from coming!"

I could hear his voice trail off as he thudded off to another room. "No! You are not coming along!"

Her own voice followed, "Oh yes I am!"

They kept going from room to room, Andy's feet stomping as he went. I sat down on the step and listened as they gradually calmed down. When it finally became silent I stood up and went downstairs. I took a deep breath and went into the kitchen. They were both sitting at the table, holding steaming mugs and looking desultory.

Andy looked up at me and winked, "Cynthia's coming with us."

I let out a short breath, "Andy, maybe you should listen to your sister. Maybe we..."

Cynthia's head popped up but Andy was short and sweet, "You gave me your word Zachary."

It was my turn to mumble, "Well, I didn't exactly..."

"It's all settled Zachary. We're going." He turned to his sister, "We're all going."

Cynthia stood up, "Well, since it's settled, may I make a suggestion?" She didn't wait for his permission and said, "We have a nice supper, go to bed and make an early start tomorrow."

Andy sighed, "I wanted to go tonight."

I said, "No, your sister's right. Let's do that."

I turned to her with a smile but she only smirked in reply and then went to the fridge and took out some pork chops.

Andy smiled, "The clothes fit. Lookin' good."

"Yeah, um, thank you."

Cynthia turned, "I can't believe you bought him clothes!"

Andy lifted his palm to her and sighed wearily, "No more arguing."

She turned back to the counter to fix dinner while Andy and I sat at the table smoking and exchanging little smiles and chuckles as the tension began to ebb. Cynthia was the only one who spoke while we ate and it was mostly to herself. Saying things like, "I have to call the hospital. Then there's Mrs. Daneko, maybe she can take care of the house while we're gone. I have to get a hold of Clarice and let her know."

During the meal, Andy got up to go to the bathroom and Cynthia levelled very cold eyes at me and said, "Andy has a gift. He can see what's inside people. He likes you and he trusts you."

I smiled warmly.

She practically growled the next words out. "I don't have that gift. Consequently, I don't like you and I don't trust you."

"Look Cynthia," I said in an attempt in a placatory tone, "None of this was my idea. He begged me to come…"

She cut me off with another snarl. "I don't want to hear it. The only thing you need to know is that if you hurt or take advantage of Andy in any way, I'll kill you."

You know how when most people say, "I'll kill you" they mean that they'll get mad at you, or in a worst case scenario, beat you up... well, when Cynthia said it, I believed that she was being literal. Not only did I think she would actually kill me, but that she would take great pleasure in doing it. Before I could frame an adequate response Andy came back and Cynthia went back to eating as if she hadn't threatened to end my life.

After dinner she left Andy and I to clean up. He wrapped up the leftovers while I loaded the dishwasher and then after another cigarette, we went back to the car to finish unloading his recent purchases.

Along with the clothes, he bought me a pair of expensive running shoes and even a dark grey double breasted suit that I could tell would be way too big for me. Nevertheless, I thanked him profusely because he watched me eagerly as I inspected each item. He helped me pack up all the clothes in two suitcases that he had dragged up from the basement and when we were all done it was about nine o'clock. He looked around to see if he had forgotten anything and then gave a nod of approval.

"Tomorrow the real adventure begins."

I nodded, "Yup."

"And what with Cynthia coming..." He winked at me, "Who knows?"

I pretended that I didn't get his meaning but somehow I knew that he had planned for Cynthia to come along right from the start. He looked at me shrewdly and then laughed, closing the door behind him as he left.

Day Three

Tuesday the Twelfth

Don't you just hate those people who tell you about their stupid dreams? I think there are maybe seven people in the world who actually want to hear about them. The rest of us hate it, but we always get sucked in when the person baits you with, "I had the weirdest dream... and YOU were in it!" So of course we listen to the inane dream only to find out that we show up near the end and don't do anything except stand around.

"Oh my GOD, did I tell you about the WEIRDEST dream I had last night? I was running and running..." Why do people always run in their dreams?

"I was running from this guy and it turned out that it was my DAD! Only my dad became a DOG! Can you imagine? Anyway, I was RUNNING and THEN...." It drives me nuts. Don't you just absolutely hate it?

Too bad, because I have to tell you about the dream I had the night before we left for California.

I was sitting in Andy's Mercedes and I was alone on this deserted highway. It was the middle of the night and I was going a hundred and fifty miles an hour. I know because I looked down at the speedometer and the needle was close to being buried on the right hand side of the gauge. The yellow line was steady on my left and there was absolute blackness all around me except for the yellow line illuminated in the glow of the headlights. Then the car started to shimmy and shake and then all of a sudden...

That's it. I woke up because Cynthia was shaking the bed with her foot.

I know that seems pretty boring and you could tell me about twenty dreams that you had that were way better and even had naked people in it but I don't want to hear about it because I wasn't in any of them.

Anyway, I opened my eyes and felt the bed moving underneath me. I looked up and saw Cynthia leaning over and shaking the bed with her foot, like it would kill her if she actually touched me. I felt like I had leprosy. Really beautiful people often do that. They make you feel like you have some vile communicable disease and they would get it if they came too close or God forbid, touched your arm to wake you like any normal plain looking person would.

Once she saw I was awake she took a step back and said in her annoyed voice, "Get up. We're about ready to go."
I rubbed my eyes, "OK."
She was staring at me with cold loathing and she said, "Just in case I didn't make myself clear last night, I don't like you."
I squinted at her through my morning fog, "Fine, I don't like you either."
"I don't like you and I don't trust you."
"OK," I said, "I think that's been firmly established. Do you want me to write this down so you don't have to keep saying it every time we see each other?"
"No need, if I get the feeling that you forgot, I'll remind you again."
I looked at her and wondered if there was anything that I could say but I knew that I couldn't appease her, even if I wanted to.
She kept looking at me with a sneer and she said, "I'm keeping my eye on you."
"Great, wonderful. I feel so honoured."
"And Andy told me to remind you to have a shower."
I chuckled, "Your brother sure has a thing for showers."

I wasn't quite prepared for her outburst, "Don't you bad mouth my brother!"

I gave her a look to remind her that she was nuts, "I wasn't bad mouthing him. Man, are you ever touchy."

Her flawless skin turned pink in anger, "I am NOT touchy! I just don't think you have any right to say that kind of thing about Andy! Not after he bought you all those clothes and is paying for your trip!"

It was obvious that Andy hadn't told her about the hundred grand otherwise she would have woken me with a cattle prod. I wasn't about to tell her either but I stayed on the defensive.

"Hey, I was the one who risked life and limb to help him at the grocery store!"

She didn't get a chance to answer because Andy was right behind her, "That's right Cynthia, he did. So get off his case." He came around his sister and clapped his hands at me, "C'mon! Time to get up!"

I started to lift the sheet but I paused and looked at Cynthia, "Would you mind leaving?"

She let out a short, harsh laugh. "I've seen boys in their skivvies before."

I imitated her laugh, "I'm sure you have."

Her face contorted into a look of supreme disgust and Andy almost fell over laughing as she stormed out. I couldn't help feeling a little bit pleased with myself.

Andy was still chuckling as I got up and he said, "This is going to be the best trip ever!"

I rolled my eyes, "Yeah, the three of us crammed in a car together for two thousand miles. Big fun."

He grinned, "Don't worry, she'll grow on you."

I glared at him, "She hates my guts!"

"Nah, she doesn't hate you." He paused, like he was reconsidering. "She'll come around." He looked up to the ceiling, "Besides, it's all in the plan."

"What the hell are you talking about?"

"The plan! There's always a plan!"

I picked up my clothes and said, "Y'know, you make these great sagacious comments like you have a direct line to Heaven but you're only full of it."

He grinned sagaciously as he headed for the door, "Go have your shower."

He was out in the hall and I called after him, "And what's with you and these damn showers?"

When I finished my shower and got dressed Andy was waiting for me at the foot of the stairs with a cup of coffee. "Drink up; I want to be on the road in ten minutes."

I sipped the coffee and stood around like an idiot while Andy and Cynthia buzzed around getting all the last minute things done. As I stood and watched the frenetic activity I realised that Cynthia had three different moods when she was around Andy and all of them were motherly in one way or another. One was the typical worrywart, constantly fretting over runny noses and dirt on brand new shirts. The second was the foaming at the mouth angry mother who thinks everything her son does is idiotic, dangerous and likely to lead to a prison term. The kind of mother that thinks that she can guide her son onto the right path by yelling like a baboon and threatening corporal punishment with a rolling pin. The third, and most annoying of all, was the mother who wants to be confidante, friend, and over all chum to the fruit of her womb. The kind of mother who tries to be all hip when her son brings his friends around and ends up mortifying everyone within earshot by using teenage vernacular like "oh, snap!"

In direct contrast to these schizophrenic characters was the way she treated me. She was a complete bitch. No wavering at all; just one steady stream of bitchiness. She may have been the reason that I decided to sleep over the first night but that was before I got a taste of her personality.

Do you remember that fairy tale about the Billy Goats? It's the one where they're trying to cross this bridge but there's this troll that lives under it. Cynthia was the troll. Every time I got a flash of her lunatic eyes I thought that nothing would make her happier than sitting under a smelly bridge and eating goats.

"Maybe you could help instead of just standing around drinking coffee."

Baaaah.

Andy walked past carrying a suitcase, "Leave him alone, we're just about done."

The car was loaded about five minutes later and the three of us gathered on the driveway for a final look around. Andy tossed me the keys, "Alright, let's get this show on the road."

Cynthia glared at me, "You better drive carefully, this is a ninety thousand dollar car."

I flipped the seat forward for her, "Good thing you'll be close by to point out any moving violations."

Andy laughed and Cynthia turned her attention his way, "Do you have your motion sickness pills?"

Andy frowned, "Yes I have them. Just get in the car."

We all piled in and I started the car. Andy clapped his hands together, "Whither goest thou America, in thy shiny automobile?"

"Huh?" Cynthia and I said in unison.

"On The Road! Jack Kerouac!" He pointed at me, "You're Sal Paradise and I'm Dean Moriaty!"

Cynthia jumped into her bosom buddy mode and leaned forward against Andy's seat. Her voice became all chummy and innocent, "Who am I, Andy?"

He grimaced, "You're just some chick along for the ride." He patted the dashboard, "OK Sal, let's do it!"

I put the car in reverse and we were off on our great and glorious journey. Almost.

There was a brief stop at a nearby Macdonald's along with a spat about who ordered the damn Egg Mcmuffins and why the hell they always make the coffee so hot. Then we stopped at a gas station to fill up and Cynthia had to use the bathroom again like some incontinent grandma.

When we finally made it to the city limits the highway loomed provocatively before us and I slipped it into fourth, feeling the pavement tear away.

For the next twenty miles Cynthia let loose a steady barrage of classic back seat driver maledictions. I gripped the wheel with white knuckles as Andy tried to suppress the laughter that was welling up deep in his belly. Satisfied that she had made her point about everything having to do with vehicle operation she slipped on her headphones and picked up a book of plays by Oscar Wilde.

As soon as her nose was in the book I flipped her the bird and the bubbling cauldron of laughter erupted from Andy, making him squirm and bob in the seat. Cynthia looked up for a moment, shot us both a dirty look and then returned to her book.

Andy's plan about the two of us getting to know each other went into full swing. He started giving me his opinion of everyone that we passed in the right lane. What I learned the most in the first hour on the road was that not only did Andy have a vast and eclectic taste in music but also a terribly short attention span. He would pop in a CD, click the button seven or eight times to find the song he wanted and then listen to about thirty seconds before putting in another CD and repeating the process all over again. What with his squeaky voice singing loudly and terribly off key I was ready to swing the car into the oncoming lane. What made it even worse was that he got all the lyrics wrong and I had to finally give his hand a resounding slap after the tenth CD. He took the reprimand gracefully; rubbing his hands and singing even louder.

It was a peaceful drive, with sunny skies and barely any traffic. Cynthia would take breaks from her book and remove her headphones to look out the window with little wistful sighs. I kept looking at her surreptitiously in the rear view window and it was those times when she wasn't talking that I could have fallen in love with her at the drop of a hat.

Andy seemed content to do his solo sing-a-long as he leaned back in his seat with half closed eyes. I started to feel really good about the trip and I daydreamed about Cynthia on the beach wearing a string bikini and a piece of duct tape over her mouth.

The traffic got heavier once we neared Calgary but we didn't stop once and the trip through town lasted less than twenty minutes. On the freeway, a cherry red Trans Am was right behind us and once the car got close enough for the two young male occupants to get a look at Cynthia, they wouldn't budge.

To her credit, Cynthia ignored the wolf calls for almost thirty seconds before she gave them the finger. Daring young suitors that they were, they remained undaunted. They even went as far as pointing out that the two dorks in the front ought to be dumped off somewhere so she could be with a couple of "real men".

Andy and I started to yell back unflattering observations about them and when the freeway turned into the highway, our two cars were swaying in our respective lanes at seventy miles an hour. We had our windows down and we had to practically scream to make sure our insults were getting their due attention.

The speed steadily increased and Cynthia turned her gaze away from the two goofs toward the speedometer that was now reading eighty-five miles per hour.
"Slow down dammit!"
"Shut up!" Andy and I yelled.

We exchanged the lead with the red sports car as we bobbed in and out of the traffic that was leaving the city. In no time at all Cynthia was frantic and Andy looked happy enough to wet his pants. Even the two guys beside us were no longer concerned with Cynthia as they cheered and yelled and waved their arms at us, egging us on to further death defying speeds.

"Blow their doors off!"

Ninety-five. I switched lanes so fast the CD skipped.

"Slow down!"

"Shut up!"

One hundred. I swerved around a station wagon.

"Slow this car right now!"

"Race 'em all the way to the border!"

One fifteen. The engine roared as I overtook a rusty pickup.

"Stop the car!"

One twenty. The guy in the four-door sedan looked like he was going to have a heart attack as we breezed past.

"Woooo!"

One thirty and the Trans Am faded into the distance.

"I swear to God I'm going to puke!" Cynthia's moan told me that she meant it.

"Me too!" Andy's cheerful reply seemed just as sincere.

One thirty five and the Trans Am was nowhere to be seen.

Cynthia leaned forward with her head between her knees and made a retching noise.

One twenty.

"Hey! Why are you slowing down?"

One ten, another retching noise.

One hundred, ninety-five, ninety, eighty, seventy, sixty and the car was silent and filled with the unmistakeable odour of vomit.

Andy turned in his seat, "Hey Cynth, are you ok?"

"Ah'm gonna..." Another retch, "...Kill you both."

I slowed the car to fifty and said, "Uh, should I stop?"

Cynthia's voice was dry and her words scratched my eardrums, "What do you think, idiot?"

I pulled over onto the shoulder and shut the car off. The three of us got out and I tried to avert my eyes from the brownish stain directly over Cynthia's pink cashmere covered cleavage.

Andy was about to say something, but his voice was drowned out by the loud roar of the Trans Am as it sped by. I couldn't make out any of the things that they yelled at us but I could imagine any number of unflattering things that it might have been.

Cynthia stood at the side of the road glaring at Andy and me for a solid minute before she opened the door and muttered something about having to clean up the mess.

"I'm really sorry." I said, not meaning a word of it.

"Me too." Andy said, again with as much sincerity.

"Screw you both." came the earnest reply.

Andy said, "There's a gas station up ahead, we can stop up there and clean the car out."

I was worried that Cynthia's glare would never leave, "You mean you two can clean up the mess! I'm the victim; I shouldn't have to clean anything!"

Neither Andy nor I wanted to argue so we all got back in the car and drove the short distance to the gas station. Andy kept looking over at me with a tight-lipped smile that warned me that he was going to have another laughing fit as soon as his sister was out of earshot.

I drove around back to the water pump and we all got out again. Cynthia grabbed one of her three bags of clothes from the trunk and slammed it shut. I grabbed the water hose and opened the back door, retreating a couple steps because of the smell. I said, "Geez Cynthia, this is a ninety thousand dollar car. Try to be more careful."

Andy's tittering exploded once again and Cynthia turned for the bathroom in a huff.

By the time she emerged wearing a whole new outfit and freshly applied make up, Andy and I had cleaned out the mess, filled the tank with gas and hung about ten of those pine tree deodorizers in the car.

Before she got in, Cynthia took a tentative sniff and said, "I'm dead serious now; if you guys pull anything like that again I'll circumcise the both of you with a rusty pitchfork."

Andy let out a giggle but I had hoped that when the subject of my private parts came up that she would have been in a more supplicating mood.

The memory of the past few miles, as well as the faint odour that remained, had turned us all off on having lunch so we planned to have dinner after we crossed the border.

We were all in a somewhat subdued frame of mind after we left the gas station. At least Andy and I were. Cynthia was still far from cheerful and made snarky little comments every couple of minutes, which I did my best to ignore. Unfortunately, being magnanimous is definitely not my strong suit so I returned the comments with some snarkiness of my own. It didn't take long for the witty exchange to turn nasty and we were yelling ourselves hoarse until Andy demanded silence in a high, shrieking yell. Cynthia and I settled for exchanging dirty looks.

Andy took his turn at the wheel as I reclined in the passenger seat, stinking up the car with Turkish cigarettes. Of course Cynthia complained about that too but no amount of cursing and threatening were about to keep me from one of my favourite vices.

We drove the seam where the mountains met the plains and Cynthia even shut up for a few minutes as we admired the view. The Rockies loomed imposing and eternal to our right and the plains stretched out comforting arms on the left.

I should have told you right from the beginning that I'm the worst person for describing things. I wish I could do the scenery justice but trust me, it really was majestic and I'm mad at myself for not conveying the sublime image to you. Go see it for yourself, and then you'll know. If I could offer one piece of advice it would be to take the trip without a whiny blonde in the back seat.

We made it across the border without any delay other than the usual bureaucratic nonsense. The custom officials were polite enough but I wish I could find someone who can satisfactorily explain to me the significant danger of citrus fruit.

I mean, I can see the point in not allowing firearms. American criminals hate competition. Ha, ha. I also understand prohibiting narcotics, rabid dogs and kidnapped, underage white slaves... but citrus fruit? I guess those are the educational things that you eventually pick up when travelling in foreign lands.

We drove for a couple more hours, keeping our bearing south, and as Andy put it, a little to the right. We passed a few eateries until we settled on a diner named "Tex's", which, I imagine, is the sister restaurant to "Montana's", located in Texas. We decided to stop there because by that time, faint vomit odour or no, we were all pretty hungry. Also, Cynthia picked it because she thought it looked "cute". I didn't catch any of the cuteness of the diner itself, but the waitress wasn't bad looking. She gave us all a big smile and took our orders without the benefit of a pen and paper. Stuff like that always impresses me because I can't remember a phone number three seconds after someone tells it to me.

Men of the world that we were, Andy and I ordered steaks seeing as we were in "cattle country". Cynthia ordered the Lasagne. What a hick.

About midway through the meal Andy pulled out the road map and set it down on the table. He pushed aside the ketchup, napkin holder and salt and pepper dispensers so he could unfold it. I moved my coke aside and when he had the map opened he popped a french fry in his mouth and mumbled, "We should make Idaho in no time at all. I figure a couple hours and then we're in the potato state!"

I wrinkled my eyebrows, "Isn't Ohio the potato state?"
Cynthia leaned over the map, "It's Iowa you idiot."
Andy took a sip of his drink, "Well it's one of them anyway."
I said, "I'm pretty sure it isn't Idaho."

"Well what is it then?" Andy asked.

I shrugged, "I dunno, Buckeye state?"

Cynthia said, "What's Ohio?"

Andy had another fry, "It doesn't matter, we're not going there."

Cynthia glared, "None of this matters anyway! Who cares what they call it!"

Andy smoothed out the map, "Anyway, we'll be in Idaho if we keep on going today."

Cynthia shook her head. "I'm not staying cramped up in that car for another hour. I say we stop here tonight and get a fresh start in the morning."

Andy frowned, "I wanted to be in Vegas by tomorrow."

Cynthia made a face, "You never said anything about Vegas!"

I for one thought Vegas would be cool.

"Vegas will be so cool!" Andy exclaimed.

Cynthia knew Andy's word would be law since this was his trip but she played the sympathy card. With a frown she said, "Andy, I don't really want to go to Las Vegas."

He toasted her with a ketchup laden French fry, "Too bad."

Her frown switched back to her crinkled brow witch look, "Too bad? There are three of us here! I say we vote!"

She turned to me and smiled. The manipulative troll.

I smirked, "I vote for Vegas."

Andy's smile was victorious and even a little gracious, "Two to one."

Cynthia spat out, "Screw two to one. I don't want to go."

Andy said, "Well I didn't want you to come in the first place but I gave in."

It was up to me to be the peacemaker so I tried my best smile on Cynthia, "It'll be fun."

She looked at me like I had just grabbed her butt, "Oh screw you." She threw down her napkin, "Ok, we'll go to Vegas but I'm not going another mile today." She stood up, "I have to go to the bathroom and by the time I get back you two can decide all on your own which hotel we'll be staying at."

She stalked off and I turned to Andy, "That woman is so charming."

He chuckled, "You'll really see it when we tell her that we're at least ninety miles away from a hotel."

"Staying in a Super Eight will do her some good."

He laughed, "We won't find out tonight. I think our best bet is that flea bag motel we passed about a mile back."

I smiled, "Thank You God."

A half an hour later Cynthia took one look at the motel and sneered, "So much for five star accommodations."

Andy hoisted his suitcase out of the trunk, "A bed's a bed."

I nodded, "Good enough for me."

Cynthia turned to me, "Well that goes without saying."

I returned the mocking smile and grabbed my own suitcase.

Cynthia said, "I'll go get the rooms." Andy handed her his credit card and she flicked a strand of hair out of her eyes and marched off toward the office.

I watched her cute butt wiggle as she walked away but when I felt Andy's eyes on me I turned away, "Nice night."

He looked up with a smile, "Lots of stars out tonight."

"Yup, this is what they call God's country."

His eyes swept down to meet mine, "The whole planet is God's country."

He looked dead serious so I looked back to the sky, "It's just an expression."

"Doesn't matter. It's the truth. We're the strangers here."

"Yup, we're a motley trio of tourists."

"No, I mean all of us. Everyone. We're all strangers and pilgrims. We make such a big deal about our lives, worrying and fretting and working our butts off. We don't really belong and our harvest is dust."

I looked back to him and saw that he was staring up to the sky as well, "Zachary, the closer I get to death the less it bothers me."

I didn't know what to say so I didn't say anything.

He kept his head back but he looked at me, "What do you think? Is the Tao a river or is it only like one?"

I chuckled, "Andy, I don't have a clue."

He smiled, "I don't know the answer either. All I know is, when I come to a river, the first thing I do is look for a bridge."

I pondered that for a moment, "That would make sense. But I still don't have any idea what you're talking about."

The smile grew deeper, fully exposing the two gaps in his dental work. "You will Zachary. You will."

Cynthia reappeared holding two keys attached to two big wooden handles. She held one out to Andy and kept the other one.

"Where's mine?"

She turned to me with a really smug look, "Since you and Andy are all for one on everything I figured you two could bunk together."

Andy smiled brightly, "That's fine." He tried to conceal his happiness, "It's only for one night anyway."

I had a lot to say to Cynthia but I kept quiet, not wanting to get into another argument before bed.

We picked up our suitcases and headed to our respective rooms. I was the first in the bathroom and I was out of there in less than two minutes. As soon as I got out Andy jumped in and I heard the shower going within ten seconds.

I got undressed and into the bed that was furthest from the bathroom. I wasn't too keen on staying in the same room with Andy because I was pretty bagged and I wasn't in the mood to stay up half the night listening to him and his inexhaustible supply of energetic banter.

I kept the light on as he had his shower so he wouldn't break a scrawny leg on the night table. I lay there listening to him sing in the shower for almost half an hour before the water finally shut off. I could hear him brushing his teeth and gargling and walking around on the squeaky floor.

He opened the door, letting out a Mt. St. Helen's sized cloud of steam. He went over to the light, turned it off and got into bed.

After a few seconds he let out a long breath, "Zachary?"
"Yeah?" I mumbled, as I feigned extreme exhaustion.
"Idaho IS the potato state."
I flipped over onto my other side, "Good night Andy."
I could hear his smile, "G'nite Zachary."

DAY FOUR

Wednesday the Thirteenth

As I mentioned earlier, I can usually sleep anywhere without any trouble, but that night I think I slept maybe two hours. When Andy wasn't snoring to beat the band he was awake, pacing the floor and humming songs like he had mixed speed in with his coffee. If you think it isn't annoying as hell waking up to see a red head pacing the floor in his boxer shorts and humming a song then you're nuts.

I'm not talking about lullabies either. He was humming songs from various heavy metal has beens, huffing and puffing the guitar riffs the way people who have no musical talent do. "Dywu, dyu, ayh, aynh." It almost made his snoring peaceful.

Consequently, I was in a rotten mood when the night was finally over. Andy, on the other hand, was a picture of joy; ready to take on the world and not give a fig whether it kicked his butt either.

He was sitting at the desk, writing away on the motel stationary and tapping the pen viciously when he paused to think. I propped myself up on my elbow and levelled my blood shot eyes at the back of his head. I plucked the biggest fruit on the sarcasm tree and squeezed it as hard as I could; "I hope I didn't keep you up last night with all my breathing."
He swivelled around to face me, "Did I keep you up?"
There was still a few drops left, "Oh no, I find air guitar at 4 a.m very soothing."
He bit down on the edge of the pen, "I'm really sorry, I haven't been sleeping too well lately. I guess tomorrow night we'll get separate rooms."
I stood up and stretched, "Good idea."

Andy turned back to his paper and I went into the bathroom to have a long hot shower. When I was done, I walked out into the room drying my hair with a towel.

Andy was reclining on the bed and he looked up at me and smiled, "I once read somewhere that ancient Samurai warriors wouldn't bathe because they couldn't allow themselves to ever let their guard down. Hot water was too relaxing and if they relaxed, they wouldn't be prepared to ward off the attack of some other strung out Samurai." He giggled, "Those guys must have been totally stressed."

I threw the towel back into the bathroom, "Is that why you like showers so much? Because you're waiting for your big chance to get your ass kicked by a Samurai?"

His chuckle disappeared as he looked past me to the bathroom. "Are you just going to leave that towel there?"

I went over to my bed and pulled out my suitcase, "Yup."

He didn't say anything for a few seconds and then he got up and went into the bathroom, presumably to tidy up after me.

His voice echoed slightly from the bathroom, "Cleaning ladies have a tough enough job without people just throwing stuff around."

"That's what they get paid to do!"

"Yeah, but why make it harder on them?"

I looked over at his bed and noticed that it was made, complete with hospital corners.

"They have to change the sheets y'know!" I said to the bathroom.

"I got the fresh sheets before you woke up!" He came out of the bathroom, "Hurry up and make the bed so we can go get some breakfast."

I scoffed, "I'm not making the bed."

He pointed to the chair next to the window, "But I got clean sheets for you too."

"Oh really?" I said as I slammed my dirty clothes into the suitcase and zipped it up.

He went over to my bed and stripped the covers off, "Just imagine how happy the cleaning lady will be when she comes in here and sees that she doesn't have to do anything."

I sat down at the chair, put my feet up on the desk and lit a cigarette. He was putting on the new sheets and I had to remark to myself just how much of a nut he was sometimes.

"I know you think I'm some kind of a nut but if you were a cleaning lady..."
I sat upright, "That's really starting to freak me out!"
He stopped putting on a pillow case and looked at me, "What?"
"You've done that like fifty times!"
"Done what?"
I stood up and pointed my finger at him, "You know exactly what I'm talking about!"
He spread his hands out, "I don't have any..."
"You're...psychic or something!"
He laughed.
"I was just sitting right there and thinking you were a nut and then not two seconds later you said, "I know you think I'm a nut.""
He shook his head, "You're crazy."
"The exact same thing happened yesterday! I was thinking that Vegas would be cool and then you said it!"
He wrinkled his eyebrows, "Coincidence."
"It happens all the time!"
He shrugged, "Maybe you're just easy to read." He snapped his fingers, "Maybe we just think alike."
"Oh please!"

He looked at me the way we look at our crazy grandparents when they go off on some Alzheimer induced tale about Coney Island cotton candy or something equally loopy. He wouldn't say anything and then I began to think that maybe I was going crazy.

"I don't think you're crazy or anything but..."

"You just did it again!"

He started for me, walking slowly, like a psychiatrist trying to get a guy to step away from a ledge.

I backed away, "I swear to you Andy, you're freaking the hell out of me! Now tell me straight out, are you a... a..."

"A psychic? A mind reader? Someone with supernatural powers?"

"Yes! Tell me!"

"OK, yes, I am."

"Don't tell me that!" I screamed. "I don't want to hear it!"

"Relax, I can explain everything."

"I don't want to hear it!" I almost put my hands over my ears and started humming.

He smiled, "OK, I won't tell you, but you have to relax. We need at least one sane person on this trip."

I took a deep, deep drag from my cigarette and let it out in shaky wisps, "It's just really weird. It's uncanny and...unnatural."

"I thought you didn't want to talk about it."

"I don't."

I sat back down and lit another cigarette off the still burning butt. He gave me a long thoughtful look before returning to the bed and after ten seconds I felt like a complete dork.

Weird things like that have always played havoc with me. I can't even sit through a David Copperfield special; and it's not only because of his hair. Magic, mind readers, religious experiences, I hate them all. As for the big One, God, I can't even drive past a church without looking the other way.

Most people who don't believe in God came to that conclusion because they haven't seen any physical manifestations or miracles or simply because they didn't get the right answer to their prayers. For me, I stopped believing in God because I DID get answers.

When I was six years old I prayed for a new bike and the next day I got one. It wasn't even my birthday! My dad had just sold some guy a huge insurance policy and he bought me a bike. "Fire, theft, car, whole life! Here's a bike, now you can suffer eternal damnation."

He didn't really say that, but he might as well. Because having that prayer answered was too strange for me to handle. I tested it a lot of times after that too, just so you don't think I'm some kind of idiot for basing my entire spiritual life on a bike. A week later I prayed for rain and the next day it rained, even though the forecast called for sunny skies. Then I prayed that I would be the first guy picked for recess softball. I was the first one picked! I didn't even have a glove! I prayed that Susie Wallace (a hottie in the third grade) would talk to me and of course she did! She asked me if I knew which bus went to the mall. I was too stunned to speak. I also asked for new Nike running shoes (which I got later that day) and just to really test the Big Guy Upstairs, I prayed that I was taller. I know you won't believe me, but the next day, all my pants were just a teeny, tiny bit too short. I'm telling you, the Creator of the universe was really in the mood to drive me insane.

After spending most of grade two on a spiritual quest I was convinced that my prayers were being answered so there had be a God. So I stopped believing in Him. It was just too spooky. That was why I freaked out on Andy. I'm not on speaking terms with metaphysics.

Andy kept watching me out of the corner of his eye like I was about to grab a knife and go after him. I decided that maybe I owed him an explanation and I didn't want him to fear for his life so I told him the same story that I just told you.

He answered in typical fashion, "That is the dumbest thing I've ever heard."

I glared, "See if I ever tell you anything personal again."

"No, I mean, how can you base something as momentous as belief in a Creator on a new bike and a rainy day?"

"I had to test it."

"But God passed the stupid test. I mean, He basically proved His existence to you which is way more than He does for most people."

I didn't answer as I was busy mulling that over.

"And after it was pretty clear that God existed..." He continued, "You stopped believing?"

"I didn't say it made sense, it's just what I believe."

"You don't believe in God because you believe in God."

"Exactly."

"This is like a Buddhist Koan. Let me try to figure out this paradox."

"Don't bother."

He gave me a long hard look, "You're completely illogical."

"Oh, and you're not?"

"No, I'm not. I follow things through by logic."

"Like instigating a fight with two goons in a grocery store?"

His enigmatic smile came like it was just waiting for me to bring up that example. "Exactly like that. If I hadn't done it you and I wouldn't be here right now."

"And this is a good thing right?"

"Don't be so snide, you know this trip is just what you needed."

"So you had all this planned out while standing in the express lane? Whatever you say Swami."

He jutted out his chin, "I never said I planned it all out."

"You said you follow things through by logic. That means you planned it all out from the beginning with that fight at the store."

"I never said that I was the one who planned it. I just followed along because it's logical to obey God."

I stood up, "Enough. I'm not about to get into a theological argument with you and if you plan on bringing this up again I'm catching the next plane home. Understood?"

He sighed, "Fine. But I wasn't the one who brought it up in the first place."

"Whatever! This conversation is over and if you're done playing Molly Maid can we go get some breakfast?"

He answered by smoothing out the bed and picking up his suitcase. He walked past me and held the door open, looking at me expectantly.

I stood up and smiled, "The long and winding road beckons." That made him smile and I felt much better because of it.

Andy went into the office to pay the bill and I leaned against the car, smoking another cigarette and trying not to think about God, my unusual predicament and life in general. Cynthia emerged from her room looking radiant as usual. She plopped her suitcase down next to the car and I stood up straighter, "Good morning."

"Don't try to be civil with me." She said.

"Excuse me?" I replied, a little taken aback.

She stared at me with cold eyes. "What's your deal anyway?"

"What?" I was starting to get frustrated that she had me at such a loss.

"Why are you here?"

"Why am I...?"

She let out a whoosh of air. "Why are you on this trip? Are you trying to get something out of my brother? Or are you attempting to make face time with me?"

I almost sputtered in frustration, "Face time with you? Are you kidding?"

She brushed her hair back from her forehead, "I'm only saying..."

It was my turn to take the offensive. "You really think I walked away from my life to go on a cross country trip with complete strangers because I wanted to "make face time with you"" (I even did the finger quoting thing. That drives people nuts.) "Are you really that high on yourself that you think...?"

"OK, I get it." She snapped. "But you still didn't answer my question. Why are you here? For a free vacation?"

"Maybe."

"Are you really that pathetic? Don't you have any friends of your own?"

I really didn't know how to reply to that because as you know the answer. Thankfully Andy emerged from the office and Cynthia let the matter rest. The three of us got in the car and headed the short miles toward the diner that we had eaten supper at the night before.

Andy drove, Cynthia was in the back and I sat in the passenger seat thinking how Andy was nothing but an ugly red headed freak and probably had fantasies about big burly men. I was trying to test Andy, maybe out of surliness towards his sister but also because I wanted to finally see if he could read minds all the time.

He didn't react. He kept his eyes on the road and hummed the song that was playing on the radio.

Then I thought to myself that he was stupid, a liar and smelled really bad. His sister was a skank and I should have let those two guys at the grocery store beat the hell out of him.

Still nothing. I stared right at him but his eyes never wavered and the humming continued without pause. I tried to think as loud as I could. I thought slowly and clearly; every word was articulated perfectly but Andy never blinked. I even tried thinking some complimentary thoughts about him but still nothing. After the two miles had passed, it hit me how ridiculous I was acting. I swear, I thought I was the biggest dork alive.

All of a sudden the bastard smiled! I really was losing my mind.

We pulled into the diner parking lot and filed into the nearly deserted restaurant. Aside from a waitress, the cook and the three of us, there was one guy drinking coffee at the counter.

Once again Andy had the map out and was trying to calculate how long it would take us to get to Vegas. Cynthia leaned forward and whispered to her brother, "Let's get out of here, that guy at the counter keeps looking over."

Andy and I both turned to look at the guy but he was hunched over his coffee, reading the newspaper.

I said, "He's reading the paper."

"He was looking at me two seconds ago."

Andy shrugged, "He isn't now anyway."

"Well he was."

I laughed, "You think every male is ogling you." I was still pretty choked about her treatment of me that morning and I was spoiling for a fight.

She made that exceptionally unattractive face, "I don't think that EVERY male is looking at me, just THAT one."

"Who cares? Let him look then."

"I care. It isn't fun being leered at all the time!"

"You're the most egotistical chick I've ever met. You think every guy wants you."

"Who the hell do you think you are? You can't talk that way to me."

She looked over at Andy for support but he kept his eyes on the map in front of him.

"I can talk to you anyway I like because I'm an emissary for my gender and on behalf of the male population I'd like to inform you that you are NOT the hottest blonde chick to ever grace a diner."

Andy smiled but didn't say anything as he continued drawing a line from whatever town we were near to Las Vegas.

Cynthia started to get flushed again, "Listen here you little free loading snot, if you think that I'm egotistical just because I don't cave in to every cheap smile and cheesy googly eye levelled at me then you're as stupid as the rest of your gender."

I turned to my right, "Hey Andy, your sister here hates men. What's the female equivalent of misogyny?"

He didn't answer but Cynthia did, "I don't hate all men, just the ones with no class."

"Oh, and what's your definition of class? To bow down and kiss your feet?"

"No, to show respect and see people for who they are and not what they look like."

"Don't give me that. If you really felt that way you wouldn't spend an hour putting on makeup and doing your hair!"

"I do not spend an hour putting on makeup!"

"Just like you can't stop staring at yourself in every reflecting surface!"

Her face was getting red. "I do NOT do that!"

I held up my spoon, "Do you want to borrow this? You might have a hair out of place!"

"Just because you got the ugly end of the stick doesn't mean..."

"Oh, so now I'm ugly? But looks don't matter to you! People should see people for who they are and not what they look like. It's what's inside that counts, right?"

"That's right! And what's inside of you is ugly! It's ugly because you're a callous and inconsiderate jerk!"

"And you're a domineering bitch!"

We were really shouting at each other at that point and if that guy wasn't looking over before, I imagine he began to out of curiosity.

Andy slammed his hand down on the map, which made Cynthia and I jump. He turned to the counter, "Hey buddy! Were you looking at my sister?"

The guy was understandably surprised and he shook his head from side to side.

"I saw you looking you filthy pervert! If you so much as glance over here I'll come over there and make it so you won't be looking at anything anymore!"

The guy, who probably could have flossed his teeth with Andy, cast one final look over at Cynthia and I before turning back to his newspaper, sufficiently chastised.

Andy looked at Cynthia and I, "There, now it's all settled, now both of you shut up."

He straightened out the map and took a sip of coffee. "You two better learn to get along otherwise some heads are gonna roll."

Cynthia and I exchanged a look of shock that lasted a full ten seconds before we broke the ice by first smiling, then giggling and finally laughing. Andy seemed annoyed but it wasn't long before he started laughing too. We didn't laugh too long, as the bonding experience became almost a shock. Cynthia brushed a hand through her hair and said to me, "I'm going to go freshen up my make up before we go. I'll try to be done in under an hour."

I kind of smiled, and she sort of did too. It was nice actually. To be smiled at by a very beautiful woman is always nice, but getting smiled at by a very beautiful woman who you once thought hated your guts is even better.

Aside from her drop dead looks, that smile was the first redeeming quality that I had seen. The fact that she levelled that quality at me almost made my heart stop. Isn't that sad? One small kindness and I'm ready to forgive her innate bitchiness.

Friendly readers, that ought to give you a good clue as to the type of loser I really am. Aside from my bitter failure at the bush party, I never mentioned anything about my amorous liaisons. The reason why I haven't is because there haven't been too many. I've had the odd passionate tussle with a girl after a few beers but I'm no virgin or anything. I've had sex. Once.

Not that you care or anything, but her name was Denise Stillwell and I loved that cow with all my tiny heart. We were seventeen years old and we got together at one of those goofy high school dances where everybody shows up drunk in an effort to have fun but usually end up throwing up before ten o'clock.

The way I tell the story is that our eyes met and we immediately fell in love and after dancing the night away, we proclaimed our feelings by making sweet love on her parent's satin sheets.

The way it actually happened was, Denise was stoned on wine coolers and diet pills and after we stepped on each other's feet to some lame song, we went to the parking lot and did it in the back seat of her Volkswagen Jetta.

Of course, after that initial joining, she wouldn't even look at me when we passed each other in the halls. I had loved her from afar since the eighth grade but she was one of the popular "A crowd" budding debutantes and I was a shorter and skinnier version of the dork that I am today. Five years of nearly unswerving devotion rewarded with twenty minutes in the back of a tiny imported car. It hardly seems fair. I suppose I should also mention that ten minutes was spent trying to untie a knot in my shoelace so I could get my damn pants off.

I spent the next three years hating her and anyone who looked remotely like her. I felt used, cheap, and wholly unattractive. So to have a beautiful woman (even with her shortcomings in the personality department) smile at me was nothing short of a complete rejuvenation of the libido. I figured that Cynthia must have felt that sharing a laugh and a smile meant nothing, but to me, and yes I know how pathetic this will sound but I'll say it anyway... it made me feel alive.

That shrewish woman, with all her sneers and uppity attitude, made me feel like I was back in the eighth grade. Before you start laughing so hard that you choke on your gum, I have to say that I wasn't in love with Cynthia. I wasn't that bad off. I would never ever give her or anyone else the adoration that I once gave Denise. I would act the same and talk the same and if she still thought of me as donkey spit, then fine. Never again would I be hurt like a common seventeen year old. But, and a very large but it seemed to me, what if she might have feelings for me? It was too staggering to devote more than a sentence to.

Andy looked over to me and said, "Not many guys would give it to her like that."

"She deserved it." I said.

"I didn't say she didn't deserve it, all I said was that you probably took her by surprise. Guys just don't talk to her like that."

"Well," I said after a pause. "I'm sorry I was rude to her."

He smiled, "Don't be."

When Cynthia returned, with newly applied eye liner and what smelled like a generous blast of hair spray, we paid the tab and resumed our journey south, and a little to the right.

Andy took the wheel again and I was relegated to the back seat, which caused a few coarse words to fly between Cynthia and me. She won out though, not because she was right, but because after that smile, my heart just wasn't in it. It was a sunny day so we had the top down and I leaned back in the seat and closed my eyes, letting the wind blow through my hair.

The conversation was light, as we played little road trip games like naming countries in alphabetical order. My geography isn't that great but once we did it with movies and song titles I did pretty well and only got into one argument about using "Xanadu" for both categories.

I dozed off for a good hour and after seeing the first Idaho Potato State sign Andy looked at me in the rear view mirror and gave me a victorious smile. I quickly closed my eyes and pretended that I was asleep.

We stopped for a late lunch at another roadside diner but none of the clientele looked at Cynthia so we had a peaceful meal. I did notice with some consternation that Andy looked tired and he didn't speak too much during our break from the road. I asked him if he was feeling OK but he waved me off quickly and stared out the window wistfully.

"I just wish we were in Vegas. I knew we should have kept going yesterday."

Cynthia began digging around in her purse, "Vegas isn't going anywhere. We'll get there soon enough."

Andy's reply came out as a long sigh as he continued to stare out at the road.

During Cynthia's regular bathroom break I said to Andy, "What's up man? You don't seem your usual annoying self."

He smiled in a half-hearted way, "I just want to get to Vegas. I feel like something big is going to happen for us there."

I gave his ribs a playful poke, "Oh sorry, I forgot that you were a prophet."

His smile broadened, "Don't start that again."

He looked back to the window and I played around with the bacon that was left on my plate.

"You really think something big is going to happen?"

He nodded, "Yeah, something important."

"Like what?"

"I dunno."

"C'mon, you must have some idea."

He looked over to me and his eyes were tinged with red, probably from spending the night pacing the floor. "Honest man, I really don't know. It's just a feeling."

I didn't want to press him so I shrugged, "I get those feelings too."

"Really?"

"No."

He laughed, "Didn't think so."

I stood up, "I'm gonna go freshen up my make up before we go."

He laughed again, "You do that."

I went to the can and leaned on the counter, surveying the various graffiti promulgations. Cynthia's remark about me being a free loader stung a little bit and I hated to sit at the table and watch Andy pay for the meal. Watching him shell out for everything was a bit uncomfortable and I didn't even like to think about how I came along on the trip for the big hundred grand payoff.

I really was starting to like Andy and I made up my mind in that stinky john that once we got back I would refuse the money. I could accept the free clothes, lodging and meals because once we got back I would tear up the cheque and thank him for a great trip. Having made that resolution I felt a little better about having to bear the free loader tag.

After washing my hands and giving my hair a once over in the mirror I left the bathroom and made for the table but there wasn't anybody there. There was a twenty-dollar bill sitting on top of the bill and the waitress was already making her way over to clear off the dirty dishes.

I peered through the dirty window and felt a sharp thrill when I saw Andy, Cynthia and some denim-clad guy standing in front of the Mercedes. It only took me a second to see that trouble was afoot.

The guy was standing an inch away from Andy, poking his finger into Andy's chest. Cynthia was yelling and even through the thick glass I could catch the odd curse.

I practically raced to the door and flung it open. I knew that things had taken a turn for the worse because as soon as I got closer, I could hear the guy threatening to unravel Andy's cerebral cortex and Cynthia now wore a look of panic.

Without stopping, I tore right up to the three of them and pushed the guy aside. I didn't get all my weight into it and I only made him stumble a couple paces back. Positioning myself in between him and Andy, I stood up straight and said, "Anything you have to say to him you can direct to me."

He didn't answer right away as he was obviously sizing me up and I took the opportunity to do likewise. He was a little shorter than I and about the same weight but he was maybe ten years older and had probably seen a lot more fights than I had. He had really cold blue eyes that shone against his tanned face. His hair was slicked back and long at the shoulders, styled right out of the redneck truck driver handbook. His forearms were quite huge and each one bore a scarlet and green tattoo of some mythical beast.

He gritted his teeth and spat out a disgusting wad of brown tobacco, "I don't appreciate being yelled at by some punk kid so I figured I'd teach this road kill here a lesson in politeness."

Cynthia and Andy both kept their mouths shut but it seemed obvious that this guy had only been doing what came natural. Namely, shooting a glance over at Cynthia. Feeling a little brotherly protectiveness and a fair dose of lover's jealousy, I gave the trucker my best tough guy smile, "How about I teach you a lesson in how to get your ass kicked by a punk kid?"

I know what a cheesy line, but you have to understand that my adrenaline was pumping and I'm not at my wittiest under those circumstances.

The trucker, at least I was under the assumption that he was a trucker and I hope I'm not offending any rig drivers out there by insinuating that all truckers leer at girls and get into parking lot brawls. I was basing it on the fact that he wearing a Mack Truck baseball cap and there was a monster-sized rig of the same name parked nearby. My only hope is that I'm not being too stereotypical.

The trucker... OK, as a concession, I won't refer to him as a trucker anymore. I'll call him Floyd, because that was the name embroidered on his shirt pocket.

Floyd let out one of those intimidating laughs that lasted two seconds and then spat again, "You think the both of you can handle that lesson?"
"Nope," I said, "Just me."

Now, most of my fighting experiences have been of the high school variety wherein the fight, if it actually occurs, is preceded by a lot of witty retorts, insults, and a long shoving match before anyone throws a punch.

It was obvious that Floyd had been out of school for a long time because his right arm cocked back and flew forward, landing a punch right onto my nose. It was just my luck that it, meaning my nose, was still soft from the fight at the grocery store.

My blood hit the pavement at the same time my knees did but I wasn't about to lose that easy. Without thinking about pain, anguish or embarrassment, (that came after) I drove my fist at what I guessed to be his most sensitive area, and I don't mean his inability to express his feelings.

It was a great plan, except that his genitals were safely out of the way, about a foot away, to be more precise. What my malicious fist came into contact with was his knee and although it might have stung him a little bit, it certainly wasn't the deathblow that I had hoped for. My fist, on the other hand, so to speak, was pretty much useless after that so it was up to the rest of my body to attack. First I swung my leg out to kick him in the shin but Floyd seemed to be highly trained in some obscure martial art because he deftly avoided my lethal strike with a defensive move reminiscent of the great Bruce Lee. He took a step back.

The forward momentum of my kick put me in a rather awkward position and I thought that things were about to go from bad to worse because Floyd started to laugh like a hyena. Coincidentally, I was left sprawled out on the pavement like a drunken warthog and as everyone who has ever watched PBS knows, drunken warthogs are the easiest prey that the hyena ever comes across.

It was an advantageous position to be in though, as I got a good view of Cynthia kicking Floyd in his MOST SENSITIVE AREA with her... and I really do feel bad for the guy... VERY SHARP AND POINTY BOOT!

His laughter turned into a rather melodious wail that lasted long enough for Andy and Cynthia to help me up and deposit me into the back seat of the car.

Floyd was doubled over and Andy pushed him backward with one hand. He landed on the ground with a tidy thump and then my favourite brother and sister team got into the car and we drove off with the radio blasting.

I held my bloody nose with my remaining good hand, while my right fist clenched and unclenched feebly on my lap. Cynthia held out a pink handkerchief to me with a look of sympathy. I could feel my cheeks burning bright red and I fought back tears of pain, anguish and embarrassment. I took the handkerchief and pressed it against my nose, inhaling the intoxicating perfume that lingered on the fabric. No one spoke for at least ten miles as we allowed the local country station to quell the excitement with dulcet tunes of cowboy love and loss.

It was Andy that first spoke, "I think if we stop for an early night we can reach Vegas about eleven o'clock tomorrow night. Right when the action starts."

I moaned, "I think I can do without more action."

"You'll feel different tomorrow. Once you roll a few sevens at the crap table you'll be a new man."

"Good, because the old one broke."

He snickered, "You didn't break. That nose is indestructible."

Cynthia said, "Andy, that's no way to talk to him after he stepped in for you."

After hearing that I thought I was going to swoon.

Andy smiled into the rear view mirror, "My guardian angel."

I put my hand on his shoulder, "My little road-kill."

Andy laughed and turned to Cynthia, "My butch sister."

Cynthia laughed to Andy, "My troublemaking brother."

It was my turn again as I looked to Cynthia, "My bodyguard."

She smiled softly, "My friend."

DAY FIVE

Thursday the Fourteenth

When Cynthia came out of the motel she was holding three sets of keys but Andy and I stayed up late together in my room playing cards and joking around like it was a grade school sleep-over.

I don't know when it hit me, maybe during the tenth game of Cribbage or after his story about the kid next door who ate his own boogers, but at some point that night I realised two things. One, that Andy was a pretty cool guy despite his unusual behaviour and two, if I had met him, say, at school, I would have called him a geek and that would have been the end of it. We would never have ended up being friends. But that's what we became, oddly enough. Unlike friends though, he was trying to set me up with his sister.

"And did you know that she volunteers at the animal shelter two nights a week?"

Andy was still talking up Cynthia and I let out an exasperated laugh, "I already told you that I don't hate her! We're friends now!"

"She visits the elderly at the old folk's home on the weekend."

"Yeah, yeah, she's a saint."

"I'm just saying…"

"I know what you're going to say! You're going to bring up the whole "taming the shrew" thing for the millionth time! Look Andy, I like her but we just started being friends a few hours ago, don't rush things along."

He looked at me shrewdly, "You mean don't get your hopes up."

"Yeah," I said. "That's what I mean."

"But I already told you…"

"Shut up already!" I yelled and smacked him on the side of his head with the pillow.

After we batted each other around for a minute or so we broke out in laughter like a couple of pre-teen dorks. As I lay back panting I realized that I felt something that I hadn't felt in a long time: Affection for another person.

I cared about the guy, if you know what I mean. Of course you do, because there are people that you yourself care about. The reason it was strange for me to have feelings for him was because, truth be told, I'm not really a caring individual. Yeah, yeah, I can tell that you're shocked. Oh, I love my parents in that mandatory, parent-sibling kind of way and my sisters, cows that they may be, still have a place in my heart. The few friends that I've had in the past incited me to an odd burst of sentimentality but Andy, being the geeky stranger that he was, really shouldn't have meant a thing to me.

He was a profound person. He looked past appearances in that wonderful way that ugly people do. I mean, honestly, he WAS ugly and there's no two ways about it. That mop of red hair and pale skin, big bold freckles and gap toothed grin all perched atop a rail thin frame. He was a wreck, almost frightening really.

But who cares? Why can't we be like ugly people and judge others by what's on the inside? We can all agree that some of the ugliest people alive are those who have all the right moves and look damn good while they're being ugly. The beautiful damned I think some poet once called them. They have nothing inside but we worship them because of their slim waists and perfect features. Why can't we look at the world through ugly glasses? God, it's frustrating. Then again, I'm reminded that most ugly people, even though they can see the faults in the prancing beauties, still want to be like them.

But, damn it all, they're still up on us average looking people in the profound department.

It was strange to have a new best friend that I'd only known for a few days and the only thing that bothered me was the whole mind reading aspect to him. It was very late and we were both really tired and it was probably because of my state of mind that I brought it up again.

"So you can read minds huh?"

He smiled, "Are you sure you want to get into this again?"

"And you can see the future right?"

He chuckled.

"Do you do it all the time? Is that why you won 5 card games in a row?"

He laughed, "No, you're just a terrible card player."

"Seriously now."

"OK, seriously. Yes I can read minds and yes I can see the future... but not all the time. It just happens at certain times and with certain people."

I fought back my natural instincts to hide under the bed. I mumbled, "That must be the coolest thing ever."

He raised an eyebrow, "At first glance, yeah, it can be a great thing... but scary too. And the things that I do hear and see are only the things that God allows me to see and hear."

"Yeah but," I said quickly to get off the "God Topic", "Being able to read people's minds must come in handy, especially as we're heading to Vegas."

He smiled. "Maybe, but it usually doesn't work like that. I mean, it's not like I can buy a lottery ticket every time and come away with a million bucks. I only get to see what God wants me to see."

"So why are we going to Vegas then?"

He shrugged, "Maybe God wants me to see something there." He winked, "And maybe that something will bring in a few chips."

"You're the luckiest guy alive." I said, and as soon as he frowned I knew that I had said the dumbest thing ever. I mean, he was dying of a terminal disease for one thing. And all of a sudden I realized that looking the way he did, being able to read people's minds might not be the greatest gift. Who would want to read a mind that was thinking cruel things about you?

Andy nodded slowly and I saw that he knew what I was thinking. He didn't stay sad for long though, that wouldn't be Andy's style. He quickly recovered and gave me a huge smile, displaying the gaps where his teeth had once been. "It'll be a great time, Zach. For all of us."

The next morning I was so overcome with good feelings for my little ugly chum that I decided to clean up my room so the maids could have a little break. I figured that would make Andy happy and my good intentions lasted only long enough to realise that I can't make hospital corners. Those maids tuck those sheets in so well you practically have to use a crowbar to get them out and that is a skill that I am sorely lacking. So I didn't bother. I did hang up my towel though.

Back on the road, Andy was constantly begging me to go faster so we could reach Vegas by sundown. He kept telling me to pull over so he could drive but Cynthia told him to relax about a million times and when her sound advice wasn't enough, she threatened to pound him if he didn't calm down.

"If we make it there by dusk, we'll have time to change into our good clothes and make a classy entrance."

Cynthia laughed from the back seat, "What do you know about class?"

He turned to face her, "I know plenty. Number one, a classy guy never says "underwears". It's always singular. Two, when a classy guy has to go take a whiz, he doesn't say, "I have to go drain my lizard."

"So what does he say?" I asked.

"He says, "I have to go see a man about a horse."

Cynthia narrowed her eyes, "I have no idea what that even means."

"Me neither." I said.

Cynthia gave her brother a cutting look and said, "I bet you don't even know what that means."

Andy cut her off, "Do you know what else they have in Vegas?"

"Elvis impersonators?" Cynthia volunteered.

"Show girls?" I said with a big smile of my own.

"No you cheese heads. Gambling! Big gorgeous casinos filled with money for the taking!"

Cynthia leaned forward, "Oh Andy, I hope you'll be careful there. You shouldn't use your gift for…" She quickly stopped speaking and shot me a quick glance before saying, "Please promise me that you won't gamble too much."

Andy ignored her brief reference to his "gift". He just shook his head, "No way! I'm gonna break the bank!"

I said, "Do you think you're the first guy to say that? Why do you think the casinos stay open? Because they don't lose."

"Nobody else has my kind of luck."

I immediately thought about last night's revelation about how a little ugly guy with a terminal disease could figure that he had good luck.

"I'm gonna win big baby!" Andy shouted loud enough to silence my thoughts. "The casinos can clean out the conventioneers and high rollers, but they're gonna hand over buckets of chips to me! I can feel it! Lady Luck is my woman on this stop!"

"Andy, just be careful." The voice of wisdom said from the back seat.

"No, I don't have to be. Losers have to be careful, but winners can throw caution to the wind."

And on he went, boasting and bragging that the town would be dark and broke by the time he left. He was so confident and excited that my own anticipation grew as the miles tore away. The scenery was a blur on either side as the three of us perched forward like a masthead, waiting, waiting, waiting for the bright lights to explode on a dark horizon.

The last city that we had seen was Calgary, and the rural voyage whetted our appetite for urban excitement. Boise was only a green sign with an arrow, barely a temptation. Glitter Gulch was our goal. The neon strip, with its blinking lights advertising debauched dreams. The miles clicked off, the engine roared and the tires gave the asphalt parting kisses as we whisked off with stars in our eyes.

Even Cynthia, who must have been tired of third-rate bed and breakfasts, was chomping at the bit. She told us about the fabulous dress she was going to wear and what shows she was going to see. My own humble visions were of a king size bed, a luxurious bath, and being dashing and debonair as I lost my handful of chips.

The sun began to droop lazily in the west and the speedometer's needle climbed to the top of the gauge, pushing us on in fevered desire. The sun vanished and three pairs of eyes squinted beyond the headlights reach and soon enough, a glow pulsed, sending endorphins dripping in ecstatic glee. North Las Vegas was another blur as we sped forward, faster, faster and then! Las Vegas! "Welcome weary travellers!"

The strip was an explosion, a Christmas tree to our childlike eyes. Our necks craned, heads turned and fingers pointed at every flashing bulb and glittering reflection. Which hotel? Which one is the biggest? Which one is the brightest? Which one will cater to our venal desires?

I refuse to endorse any edifice; any business, any rich guy's moneymaker so suffice it to say that we picked a hotel that shall remain nameless. When you finally make it to the capitalist's Mecca, pick a hotel that gives off a good vibe. You might go to the same place we did and you may not, but damned if I'll be held responsible for making you sway in your decision by naming the hotel that we stayed at. Sorry, but this is a book about love and magic, not a travel brochure. Plus, if I did name the hotel, those jerks would probably sue me. Let me just say that this multi-storied playground was and probably still is fabulous.

It gave off a good vibe so we drove up to the curb. Andy gave the valet a twenty and three bellboys had our suitcases packed onto a dolly with lightning speed.

No reservations? No problem Mr. C Note. Three suites? Our pleasure Mr. C Note. We're at your disposal Mr. C Note and if you'll allow me, let me position myself so you can use my butt as a footstool. Anything for you, Noble and Excellent C Note. In case you missed my point, those jackals in Vegas give new meaning to the word sycophant. Seriously, if you've got the dough, they've got no reservations about sacrificing their own mothers to an Aztec deity. Not that we asked, but they would have. Trust me.

Andy handled it with a great deal of class, like he was born to hand out rolled bills into greedy palms. We were treated with something that went well beyond obsequiousness and no fooling, we all loved it. Cynthia was strutting, Andy was doing a bouncy shuffle and I was walking on a cloud. We checked into our own suites, all in a row on the twentieth floor. Andy made a stop at each door and gave each bellhop a twenty. Then, with a final joyful smile, we all stepped inside our respective palaces.

Five star baby. No kidding. It was a carpeted ballroom, man. King size bed, marble tiled bathroom, and whoa, my first stop, the fully stocked bar. I'm not much of a drinker but when I saw all that booze, my liver cringed at the same time that my mouth watered. I poured a glass three fingers full, which is to say, almost near the top, with what I think was cognac. It came in a smoky coloured bottle with a label all in French. My inexperienced palate restricts my description to saying that it was brown and it burned my throat to hell. Damn good stuff, that cognac.

I took the glass out to the balcony and looked down at the inexpressible beauty of the heated gas that lit up the city. I took another sip and the phone rang. I went back inside and answered it.

"Zachary! Put that drink down and have a shower! I want to be out on the town in half an hour!"

It was kind of weird that I was used to his psychic outbursts. "Andy, I'm not rushing for you. I've been cooped up in a car for the last three days and dammit, I'm gonna soak in that monster sized tub for the next hour no matter what you say."

He laughed, "Fine, I'll see you outside the door in exactly one hour." He hung up and I downed the cognac in one sophisticated slurp.

That tub was indeed huge and the water must have been hot enough to make a lobster scream. I loved it. I had another glass of brown and a complimentary cigar clenched between my teeth. I tell you, the only thing that wasn't just right was that the mirror wasn't low enough for me to see how damn sophisticated I must have looked. What a scene, all frothy bubbles and burning throat from the cognac and the cigar... it was a beautiful moment. Time slipped by luxuriously and I still had the nub of the cigar between my teeth when I got out of the tub. The heat and the liquor made me sway a little as I wrapped a suitcase destined towel around my waist and went out into the room.

My eyes zeroed in on the bed, or more precisely, the white tuxedo that lay upon it. I went over and picked up the little card that sat on the lapel. It was only one word, written by Andy's hand. "Class!!!!" I smiled, stubbed out the cigar in a nearby ashtray that was also going to come home with me, and put the tux on.

It fit perfectly, which was a very pleasant surprise, and I combed my hair twelve times before I looked at my watch. I slipped on a pair of shiny shoes that accompanied the tux and stepped outside. Any was already waiting, dressed in an identical tuxedo and wearing, along with his huge grin, enough gel to turn his flaming red hair glistening amber. To his left stood Cynthia, a woman to make Venus run for the nearest plastic surgeon. Dressed in a black gown with her hair up, I almost fainted out of desire. She was THE MOST BEAUTIFUL WOMAN IN THE WORLD. Sorry for the capital letters, but really, I felt like the luckiest man alive, just to be able to look at her. She stood in the middle and Andy and I each wrapped an arm in hers and headed for the elevators, giggling like the naive fools we were.

Do you remember those plastic monkeys that came in a big bucket? It was a kid's toy, remember? The whole point of the silly things was to drape them arm in arm and make this big plastic monkey chain. That was us, walking down the hall and riding the elevator. We even stayed locked together as we cruised through the lobby. Our spirits were so high and I couldn't remember ever being happier. I bet our faces were glowing to beat the neon on the strip.

We stopped at the entrance to the casino and I asked, "Should we cruise through?"

Andy shook his head, "Not yet, the Vibe isn't there. Let's go get some dinner and catch a show. Then we can go clean the bastards out."

"Should we eat here?" Cynthia asked as she looked around for the restaurant.

"No, we've got a whole city to choose from. Let's go and see what's giving out the Vibe." Andy said as he led us all toward the huge double doors that led outside.

I leaned over to him and whispered, "The Vibe? Is that what you call your voodoo mumbo jumbo?"

He grinned. "It's what I call it when we're in Vegas!"

I swear, he looked deliriously happy, a full level of happiness beyond his usual good humour.

The pavement was still giving off the heat from the scorching day so we decided to hoof it. Cynthia pointed out a few places with glowing marquees that proclaimed all star entertainment and sure-fire excitement. Andy vetoed them all, as he looked around wildly. He seemed to be sniffing a little as he pointed his nose at each place, like "The Vibe" gave off a particular smell.

We walked a few blocks, still arm in arm and drawing some stares from the casually clad gamblers and sightseers. At the end of the block Andy turned us right down a nondescript street. None of us spoke as we walked toward a marquee that stood atop a somewhat run down building. I could feel Cynthia hesitate as her walking slowed but Andy propelled us all forward.

We stopped in front and stared up at the sign. "The Ozone - Nightly Entertainment", and underneath that, "Tonite! The Song Stylings of Bobby Fabian! A special tribute to Bobby Darin and Fabian!"

Cynthia pulled her arms loose and took a step forward, blocking Andy's path to the door, "No! This place is a dump! Even the marquee is misspelled!"

Andy smiled gleefully, "It's giving me the Vibe."

"Screw the Vibe!" She could be very unladylike when she wanted to be, even in a full-length black evening gown. "I want to go to a NICE place. Eat a NICE meal. See a NICE singer, not some Fabian cover artist."

"It's Fabian AND Bobby Darin." Andy corrected.

Cynthia let out what can best be described as a growl but Andy gave her his most charming and hideous grin, "Cynth, trust me. The Vibe will not lead us astray."

He stepped forward and took her elbow, leading her to the door. I looked up at the sign doubtfully and Andy paused to turn back, "You comin'?"

I shrugged, "Long live the Vibe." Then I followed them in.

The place was dark and there was no maitre d' and no coat check girl. There was a hefty looking woman of about fifty who was smoking a cigarette and she turned to us with an almost credible attempt at a smile.

"Wedding?"

A wedding party with two grooms? I knew we were in Vegas, but still…

"Um, no." Cynthia replied with a snottiness that I approved of.

The fat lady snorted and picked up three plastic coated menus and led us into the large but dank room. There were maybe twenty people in various stages of drunken glee scattered about in twos and threes, all talking in slurred mumbles and guzzling highballs. All the tables were small and we crammed around one that sat just to the left of the stage. It was lit by a fading spotlight, centred on a single microphone stand and giving us a hint that there was a sickly looking piano that sat sadly near the right hand side.

We took a quick peek at the menus and ordered stiff drinks and steaks from the ancient waitress who kind of seeped out of the gloom with a note pad. Cynthia and I exchanged shrugs as we looked around the room tentatively. Andy was leaning back in his chair, taking deep draughts of his whisky while he glanced furtively around, looking for the walking personification of "The Vibe."

Before we were half done our drinks, the scraggly old waitress informed us that her shift was over and asked if we would mind settling up the tab. It's really a bother having that happen when you've only been sitting there for five minutes and the worst thing is that you have to shell out two tips. What a scam.

We did settle up, with a hefty fifty percent tip that made Cynthia and I roll our eyes as Andy slipped it into her hand. After that we sat there like dolts with empty glasses waiting for the new waitress to arrive. I even chewed the bourbon flavoured ice cubes before a waitress named Trouble sidled up to our table.

The name on her tag may have read Cherisse, but I knew better. Anything in a leather mini skirt and a blouse cut low enough to play nipple peek-a-boo, is trouble. Trouble trouble trouble. I saw it, Cynthia saw it, but Andy saw something far different. "The Vibe." He whispered as she approached.

"So, uh, what did you people order?" Our gum chewing tart's voice was low grit sandpaper on a blackboard. Have another cigar, sweetheart. Sheesh. She was obviously peeved at having to take over another table and her attitude let off little barbs and nettles that stung my ears.

Cynthia spoke up, "What's the special?"

Cherisse let out a whoosh of aggravated air, "The buffet is all you can eat for $12.95."

"Sounds yummy." I said in a tone that was meant to convey exactly the opposite.

Cherisse's upper lip curled in a demonic smirk and Andy leaned forward on his elbows. "Could you bring me another whisky and soda?" A twenty-dollar bill suddenly appeared between his fingers. "And have one yourself."

Cherisse looked at the money, the tux and then into the eyes of our beloved Andy with a look that sharks mastered two million years ago. Even her tongue hung out a little. What a cheap skank.

All of a sudden her voice was slick with honey, "Thank you sir but I'm not allowed to drink until the end of my shift."

"And when is that dear?" Andy asked.

"Midnight." She answered with an arch of her back.

Andy placed the twenty on the table. "We'll just save this for midnight then."

She gave the money another quick glance and then smiled. It was a pure twenty-dollar smile straight out of the used car lot. I hated her. I mean I really hated her, and I'm usually only moderately repulsed when it comes to cheap skanks.

She took my order without taking her eyes off Andy and she would have totally ignored Cynthia had I not ordered the second drink before she left. She nodded and then turned to go, giving Andy a nice view of her leather clad butt.

Cynthia was on him in a second, "Andy! What the hell are you doing?"

"She's got the Vibe."

I said, "Don't you mean the Clap?"

He shot me a murderous glare, "That's enough of that. Cherisse is going to be my loving companion while we're in town."

"And you just decided that?" Cynthia demanded. "One look at pushed up cleavage and you're ready to throw money around on a hooker?"

"She isn't a hooker! She's a waitress!"

"Uh huh."

Andy waved his hand at us, "Just don't rain on my parade. Let me have some fun; that's all I ask. If you two want to go see Wayne Newton, then go now. The door is over there."

There was no way that we would ever leave Andy unattended so we settled on leaning back and looking surly.

Cherisse came back with our drinks, setting them on the table with a big bend at the waist so Andy could win the game of peek-a-boo. His eyes opened slightly and another twenty rested on the table. I thought Cherisse was going to fake her orgasm early when she saw Andy's wad of bills. I cringed and took a sip of my drink.

"Excuse me Miss. I ordered bourbon."

She looked at me with venom in her eyes, "Yes?"

"This is... I don't know what the hell this is but it isn't bourbon."

She snatched up the glass and then shot a look over to Cynthia. "Is that what YOU ordered?"

Cynthia took a sip and added in a snarky voice, "Close enough, it's in liquid form." Oh how I loved it when her snarkiness wasn't directed toward me.

Cherisse swept back her hair as she looked at Andy. "How about yours sir?" What honey, what oil, what a complete and utter cheap skank.

Andy didn't even glance at the glass, "It's perfect Cherisse, and please, call me Andy."

It was pure coincidence that I happened to be looking down at the same moment that Cynthia had the tablecloth clenched between white knuckles.

I didn't catch Cherisse's response because right after, the lights went out and the spotlight went up. Cynthia and I turned to the stage and watched the emcee, an older man with white hair, wearing a blues brothers issue black suit.

"Good evening ladies and gentlemen and welcome to The Ozone." He expected applause but after three seconds of dead silence he continued, "We're very pleased to bring you the fabulous and talented Bobby Fabian, who just finished his Middle Eastern tour and is now back in the good ole U S of A. Please put your hands together for the marvellous Bobby Fabian."

I think Andy and the five hundred pound drunk in the front were the only ones who actually clapped. The emcee hopped down from the stage and out strutted the fabulous Bobby Fabian. A forty something man with a dyed black pompadour and a bedraggled black tux that tried to conceal a purple ruffled shirt underneath. He took a deep breath and I think I caught a whiff of vermouth from ten feet away.

He went to the microphone and grabbed it with both hands, probably to steady himself after his dozen-martini dinner. "Thank you very much ladies and gentlemen. I hope you're all enjoying yourself." He plucked the microphone off the stand and walked over to the piano. "I just got back from the Middle East and let me tell ya..." He paused and looked over the crowd, "Is there anyone here from the Middle East?" After the brief silence he said, "Well," He laughed, "They're nothing but a bunch of rag head bastards!"
No one laughed but a solitary voice sprang up from the kitchen, "I'm from Syria you asshole!"
Bobby's jaw drooped a little but I have a feeling that it was from the booze and not the embarrassment. He sat down on the piano bench and said, "Well, all I can say is that it's great to be back in the greatest country in the world!"
Patriotism was dead at the Ozone that night so Bobby ended his diatribe and began a sloppy version of "Splish Splash".

To say it was the cheesiest lounge act in the history of Vegas would be unfair. Fair be damned though. It was THE cheesiest act in the history of not only Vegas, but of the entire western hemisphere, perhaps the world even. Except for the Middle East maybe, because it probably caused more bloodshed and there's nothing cheesy about that.

This Bobby Fabian joker bounced up and down on his butt as he played off key versions of some of the worst songs ever written by two teen idols. The highlight of the first set was "Mack the Knife," which was accompanied by a chorus of extremely loud belching from the table behind us. I even joined in for the first couple burps but then Cynthia pinched my leg and I let out a little yelp to Mack the Kniiiife.

Yeah, Macky was back in town and I was starting to get as plastered as the other hepcats. Cherisse made frequent trips to our table and even though the bourbon was watered down, after four or five glasses, it hardly mattered. She and Andy made what could be described as flirtatious gestures if bending over to show off boobs is considered being flirty.

Ole Bobby Fabian spotted Cynthia and began to croon "Dream Lover" to her and continued on to "Queen of the Hop" despite Cynthia's wondrous scowl. At around eleven thirty his set ended and he picked up a drink from the bar and started for our table. His big hair bobbed as he strutted over with both eyes zeroing in on Cynthia.

"Oh God, he's coming over." Cynthia moaned.

I was ready to send him packing but Andy was on his feet, clapping wildly and grinning, "Bravo Mr. Fabian! Bravo!"

With a quick wink at Andy and a smile directed at Cynthia he pulled up a chair and sat down next to her, "Please call me Bobby."

I leaned over, "How about I call you..."

Andy cut me off, "You were tremendous Bobby! Really great, man!"

Bobby took a sip of his drink and leaned back, allowing his purple shirt to nearly bust a button. He nodded, "Thanks a lot kid. I live to entertain."

Andy offered his hand, "I'm Andrew, and this is Zachary and Cynthia."

Bobby shook his hand and then turned to Cynthia with his hand poised. "Hello Cynthia, I'm Bobby. But I guess you already know that."

Cynthia ignored him like he ignored me. Not that I was offended or anything, but I was looking forward to giving his hand a piano players worst nightmare of a handshake.

Bobby may have been a forty year old who never got a chance to be a has been because he was a never was. Grease seemed to ooze off him and he had that same kind of charm that is usually exhibited by drunken uncles at wedding receptions. As soon as I got a good look at him I was reminded of this kid from my elementary school named Trevor something or other. He had that same kind of idiot egotism that produced sympathy more than disdain. He used to say this line every recess: "I kill people with my knife!" Then he would produce an old butter knife from his pocket and brandish it with a fierce pride. I think he got beat up about eighty times before he made it to junior high. It was kind of sad, just like Bobby Fabian.

"And how about you sweetheart? Did you enjoy the show?"

Cynthia snarled, "I liked the end."

"You mean my finale?"

"No, when you stopped."

He laughed, "Sugar, you are spicy!"

Andy leaned forward, "Bobby, the three of us are going to rob the casinos blind as soon as my date's shift is over; will you join us?"

He kept his eyes on Cynthia, "I'd be delighted. With this lady by my side I can't lose."

Cynthia edged her chair away, "Too late loser."

I let out a giggle but it died away when Bobby laughed, "You've got spunk honey! You're a real class act."

Cynthia smiled, "Class?"

He nodded, "Real classy."

She leaned forward, resting her chin on her palms and flittered her eyelashes at him, "Speaking of class, what do you call those things that you wear under your clothes?"

Bobby looked confused but then he must have figured that Cynthia was flirting so he tried to look suave, "You mean underwears?"

Cynthia looked over at Andy and smirked, "Real classy."

Andy ignored her, "Bobby, the five of us are going to paint the town red!"

Bobby laughed, "Andrew, this town already has about five hundred coats of red. Let's paint the bastard purple!"

Andy laughed uproariously and the two men clinked their glasses in a toast before downing their drinks in one gulp.

Bobby turned back to Cynthia, "So what brings you to Vegas, muffin?"

Cynthia grabbed my hand and lifted it, "A wedding."

Bobby's eyes opened wider as he finally noticed me, "Yours?"

Smug smiles in place, we nodded in unison.

Bobby's eyes narrowed, "Where's the ring?"

My smile grew, "I couldn't afford one. You see, I just got out of prison and I've yet to kill anybody and steal their money."

Bobby didn't buy it for a second, "You guys are cards! The three of you!" He finished his drink and called out to the bar, "Hey sweet pants! Another round over here!"

He gave Andy a playful jab in the ribs with his elbow, "This waitress is hotter than a firecracker. I kid you not."

It was Andy's turn to narrow his eyes. "She's my date for the evening."

Bobby let out another grandiose laugh, "Oh, I'm just messing around with you buddy! She's a fine girl, a fine girl!"

Cherisse came over to the table and licked her lips at the pile of twenties. She placed fresh drinks on the table and balanced the tray she was holding against her hip as she looked down at Andy, "It's almost midnight."

Andy smiled seductively, "You won't turn into a pumpkin will you my love?"

Cherisse, horrible wench that she was, leaned forward so her lips were only half an inch away from Andy's ear and whispered something. It had to be something good because Andy shifted in his seat like he was just about to be called up to solve a problem on the blackboard.

Cherisse stood up straight again, "Let me go back and change and then I'll be right out."

Andy let out a dreamy sigh, "I'll be waiting."

Bobby leered at Cherisse's butt as she swayed away to the back, "Hoo baby Andrew, you got yourself a real firecracker. A real stick of dynamite. You've got class my friend."

"No Bobby! YOU'VE got class!" Andy bellowed in liquor-induced ecstasy.

Bobby had his eye back on Cynthia and when she noticed she leaned over and whispered to me, "Please don't let me be alone with this freak."

I smiled, "What? Leave my bride on our honeymoon? I wouldn't think of it."

She laughed softly and gave me a little kiss on the cheek.

I pushed my glass away. I couldn't take another drink. I was too high already from the kiss and from the smell of her hair as it fell forward when she leaned over to whisper to me. It was all pretend, I knew that. But it didn't matter. I could go on pretending for the rest of my life if she was game.

Bobby and his leering smile faded away. Andy became a blur and the noise of glasses clinking and voices mumbling were a million miles away. The only light in that dungeon came from Cynthia and the soft glow was unaware of my heart. How could I ever see her as uncaring? As a rude, selfish bitch? How? How could I mistake an angel?

My cheek tingled, it really did. It honestly doesn't only happen in the movies! I sat in that dingy dive off the strip and was in love. Grade eight infatuations be damned. Seventeen-year-old pain be accursed as well! I was in love! She kissed me and held my hand and I was in love! The background piano music played from a faraway jukebox spoke evil mysteries. It spoke that I would surely die before the night was over because there was nothing else to live for. Cynthia would never love me; even seven bourbons could not make me believe that she could ever in a million years love me.

I sat in that dingy dive off the strip and I realised that love meant death.

DAY SIX

Friday the Fifteenth

"It's got to be midnight!" Andy shouted when he saw Cherisse emerge from the back room.

She was dressed in another short leather skirt, this time red, and yet another low cut blouse. I would have loved to see her closet. How did she decide what to wear day after day?

The bill was paid quickly and I was surprised to see Bobby coming with us. "Don't you have to do another set?" I asked him.

"Nah, the boss lets me off early whenever I want."

I imagine that the four people left in The Ozone were pretty disappointed.

The five of us tumbled out of the bar and headed back to the strip. Cherisse was draped all over Andy; Cynthia held my hand (pure bliss!) and Bobby sort of bounced around like a hyper terrier looking for attention. "Yessir, I could tell you some stories about Vegas! Yessireebob!"

"Tell on Macduff!" Andy grinned as he slipped an arm around Cherisse's waist.

Bobby cackled. "I dunno if I should. It could turn that red hair white!"

We all entered the first glitz-o-rama casino and Andy made a beeline to a black jack table. Before he got two steps away Cynthia and I extricated him from Cherisse and had him out of earshot. I spoke first, "Andy, I don't think this is a good idea."

He made a wry face. "Why?"

"Look," I said after shooting a quick glance at Cynthia. "Remember what you said about, well, what you and I talked about last night? I don't think that God would want you to do this." It sounded cheesy, especially coming from a dirt bag like me but Cynthia nodded along with me. "He's right Andy. You could get into a lot of trouble."

"How? By winning a ton of cash?"

She ignored his question. "And why on earth would you get Bobby and whatshername to tag along with us?"

He glared at each of us in turn and then said, "You two can leave if you're uncomfortable. This is my destiny." Then he tore his arm loose from my grasp and stepped over to the blackjack table. He placed five hundred bucks down and bellowed, "Chips please!" The dealer handed over the chips but instead of placing a bet he led us over to one of the big wheels where two grandmas were placing their Ten Dollar chips on the table.

"I want to begin here, just to show you all that I own this town tonight! There's no skill involved with wheels, just plain dumb luck. In short, the wheels are for suckers!"

One of the grandmas turned to him, "Hey!"

"I'm sorry dear, but it's true. The casinos rake it in at these things." He grinned, "But not when I'm standing here!" He slapped all five hundred dollars worth of chips down and smiled to the grandmas, "Ride with me dearies! We'll clean up!"

They both gave him dirty looks and moved their chips further down the table.

The attendant smiled, "No more bets!" and spun the wheel. Andy didn't even look, as he turned to us with his arms outstretched, and a broad smile.

Sure enough, he tripled his money on that one spin. He winked at the old crows, "C'mon, last chance before I move on. One last bet." He kept the money where it was, "Let it ride!"

The old ladies each placed a chip down on his spot and the attendant smiled again, "No more bets" and then the wheel went in motion. Click click click click click and voila, a neat little pile of hundred dollar chips and two very happy old ladies.

"Farewell my loves!" Andy called to the cronies as we all bounded off back to the blackjack table. It was numbing; the lights and sounds and Andy, a white tux blur as he hopped over to the high stakes tables.

Bobby and Cherisse had huge smiles and they clapped their hands with each step they took. An adult carnival, but Cynthia and I weren't throwing any baseballs for prizes. We wore matching frowns and we gripped each other's hands tighter.

Andy didn't even take a seat at the table. He pushed the stool away and called for cards. A ten, a two, a six. "Stay! Stay!" I called out.

"Don't worry Zachary, I own the town." He looked at the dealer with a smile, "Hit me."

The three of hearts floated down like a snowflake and the other players exploded with cheers.

How many hands did he play at that table? Enough to make Cherisse scream and Bobby pound his back about twenty times. He never lost one hand.

After a brief twitch of his eye as if Lady Luck was whispering in his ear, he bounded off to another table. Baccarat. He won, he won and he won. Then off to black jack again. "No poker! Too slow!" He yelled as he stuffed a handful of chips into Cherisse's handbag.

Bam! Twenty-one. Bam. Dealer bust. Bam. Off to Baccarat. Bam. Hits for Player. Bam. Now Banker. Craps, roulette. Every hit was a home run and every egg golden. Bam Bam Bam and two hours had passed as we headed out the door, a five-person parade.

Cynthia and I didn't speak as we watched with increased trepidation, watching and waiting for the bubble to burst. Off to the next casino, leaving the crowds, the dealers, the croupiers and pit bosses to shake their heads and wonder about another legend of Las Vegas, shaking and rolling his way to certain disaster.

Luck turns sour and fate is fickle. Streaks end and nobody but nobody comes out of this alive. But Andy scored another huge win at the craps table and poured a heaping handful of chips into both my tux pockets. "Andy, you have to stop!"

He laughed like a man possessed and hugged me with his chin against my chest. Drinks all around and a chip stuffed into the cleavage of the busty waitress.

Another casino, as Andy was practically running down the block. We jogged after, followed by a dozen rubbernecks from the last casino. Andy was a star, taking it back for the common man. A robber baron, another Robin Hood and Billy the Kid, rolling sevens and calling aces out of the deck.

"Damn, that kid is amazing!" It seemed like the first thing Bobby had uttered in hours.

"He's mine baby! All mine!" Cherisse yelled to a blonde that was looking at Andy with a protruding tongue.

"Oh God, dear God." Cynthia said and I nodded.

How much was he up by the fourth casino and his hundredth black jack? I would have bet that it was hundreds of thousands, maybe hundreds upon hundreds of thousands. Pit bosses stayed close, arms crossed and eagle eyes looking for the cheat. It had to be a cheat. Nobody has that kind of luck and damn it all to hell; luck doesn't exist in the city that practically invented the word.

He rolled the dice and summoned sevens when he wanted them and banished them when he didn't. Twenty-One was called out in disbelieving tones. Banker wins, Player wins, he owned Baccarat. The white ball bounced where he told it to and he called up magic numbers on the roulette wheel as if he had it trained. It was madness and I felt like I was going to pass out. Cynthia was near tears, her and I being the only two people in the joint who seemed to feel a black dread.

"Can you stop him?" Her sweet whisper asked.

I only shook my head, "He's unstoppable."

Casino managers fidgeted as they waited for him to leave. The growing crowd around him cheered with every roll of the dice or flip of the card. He handed out hundred dollar chips like they were candy to the onlookers and he ran from table to table, casino to casino, winning, winning, winning. I think he gave away tens of thousands of dollars in an hour.

"He sold his soul to the devil." A man next to me murmured.

"He IS the devil!" The woman next to him joyfully exclaimed as she counted the chips that Andy had thoughtlessly pressed into her hands.

I felt a cold blast of air conditioning and almost tasted the pure oxygen. Five A.M and Andy played his pied piper tune out into the street again. Fifty, maybe sixty people followed him.

Cynthia and I found ourselves at the tail end of the procession, suddenly whipped and wanting sleep but not daring to let Andy out of our sight. The parade continued right up to the entrance of the hotel we were staying at and then all of a sudden it stopped dead, as the leader paused, scratched his chin and turned to the crowd behind him.

"That's it. The Vibe is gone. Good night everyone!"

The crowd let out a collective moan, disappointed that the show was over. I'm sure they were all waiting for him to lose. He had to and at that point I believed in the Vibe, how could I not? He would have surely lost the next hand, roll, whatever. If Andy's Vibe was gone, then it was good night everyone, and you'll have to wait a hundred years for another miracle.

Cynthia let out a sigh of relief, "Thank God."

Once the crowd saw that Andy had indeed quit, they began to drift off, in awed twos and threes, each giving him a pat on the back as they passed. Andy handed out even more chips to all of them despite the dirty looks that Cynthia and I were shooting at everyone. Andy drew Cherisse close and gave her a big kiss and then called out to Cynthia and I, who were standing about twenty feet away, "Didn't I tell you?"

Cherisse turned his face back to hers and practically inhaled his tongue. Bobby put on his tuxedo jacket that was hanging over his shoulder, "Man, that beats any story I could have told."

He gave Andy a hug around the shoulders and then said, "Kid, you made me a believer."

"Ok gang," Andy crooned, "Breakfast is on me but first let me stake you all!"

Bobby whistled appreciatively and Cherisse let out a raucous laugh. Cynthia was pale. Andy dumped a handful of chips into my pockets and I tried to step backwards but he gave me a look that said that he wouldn't accept any refusals. Bobby's pockets bulged and Cherisse surprised me by shaking her head when he offered her chips. Cynthia accepted the chips that Andy dumped into her tiny purse but as she was leaning close to say something to him, he took a step backward and shook his head.

It was just the five of us again as we went inside the hotel. The restaurant was still busy with the high rollers grabbing a bite to eat before heading back to the tables.

Andy plopped down in a booth looking pale and exhausted. "I gotta have a steak. My poor old heart needs some protein." Cherisse, who poured herself on top of him sighed, "Just a quick meal honey, then we have to put you to bed."

Andy squirmed a little as her words took effect. Bobby, who caught the meaning because it seemed his brain could understand little else, let out a raspy laugh and patted the seat next to him, "C'mon sweetie," meaning Cynthia, "Have a seat, grab a quick bite and then you and I can go and spend some of the chips that Andrew here has graciously bestowed on me."

Cynthia shook her head, "Sorry, my husband and I are going to bed."

I felt my face flush and I inadvertently gave her hand a squeeze.

Bobby grinned, "Still singing that same tune huh?"

She smirked and then bent down and kissed Andy on the cheek, "Be good Andy."

He smiled, "I always am."

Cherisse licked her lips, "I'm sure you are."

I shook Andy's hand, "You did it man, congratulations."

He smiled proudly, "Do you believe too?"

"Hell yeah, but I'm still sceptical enough to say be careful. This town is full of crooks." I wasn't going to look at Cherisse and Bobby when I said that but I did. They didn't seem to notice anyway.

"Don't worry Zachary old man, he's in good hands." Bobby grinned and then added, "As for this dog, I think I see a bone of my own." I turned around to see a hooker sitting at the counter with crossed legs and puffy red eyes zeroed in on the fabulous Mr. Fabian. He got up with a wink to all present while Cynthia and I left for the elevators.

"Do you think it's ok to leave him?" Cynthia asked with a delicate frown as she watched the elevator doors open in front of us.

I nodded, not because I was sure but because I wanted her to feel better. We stepped inside the elevator and I said, "I don't think we could have hung around much longer even if we wanted to."

She made a face, "That Cherisse has to be the cheapest trollop I've ever laid eyes on."

"Well, she has the Vibe."

She laughed, "That was funny what you said to Andy earlier. When he said she had the vibe and you said..." She put a hand over her mouth, "Oh my God, do you really think she has the clap?"

I watched the numbers on the elevator light up as we neared our floor, "That's a thought best not thunk."

"I guess so." She said reluctantly.

The doors glided open and we walked down the hall with little smiles and shy giggles that we let out for no good reason. When we reached my door we both realised that we were still holding hands.

It had felt so great being joined with her for the past five hours that her hand seemed to be a natural extension of me. It felt right but away from the other three, there was no need for any more charades. We let go of each other with another shy giggle and then she looked over at her door, "Hey, uh, are you tired?"

"No, not really." I lied.

"Do you want to come over for a little while? We can order up some breakfast from room service."

"Sounds good." I said with a nonchalant smile.

It felt strange for me to walk beside her without holding her hand and it seemed that she felt the same way because we both made short, stocky steps down the hall without knowing where to put our hands. Once inside her room, I went right over to the bar and said, "Do you want a drink?"

She threw her purse down on a chair, "I think I could use one."

She flipped off her shoes, "Make mine a cognac. Just a little though."

I nodded and poured two drinks while she went over to the phone and ordered breakfast.

"Scrambled right?"

I brought the drink over to her and nodded, "Yeah, thanks."

"And a pot of Earl Grey please." She covered the phone again, "Do you mind tea? I don't really want coffee."

I shook my head, "Tea is fine with me."

After she hung up the phone she took a small sip of her drink and sat down cross-legged on the bed. God, she was beautiful. I tried to look away and my stomach churned out of sheer nervousness. I had never been alone with her in such close proximity and I gulped my drink down loudly.

"So, you really think Andy will be ok?"

I nodded, "I think he'll be just fine. It's like he's living out some grand celestial plan."

She laughed, "He really does believe that you know."

"Do you?"

Her laugh faded, "Yes. Haven't you noticed…?"

I almost yelled, "Yes! I knew he was a psychic before he told me! We had an argument about it!"

She looked at me strangely, "He told you?"

I nodded, "Yeah, but I had him dead to rights."

"Hmmm, he's never told anyone before."

"Really?"

She nodded her head earnestly. "Did he tell you how he made our parents rich?"

"No, the only thing he told me is that..." I brushed an imaginary piece of lint of my pants, "Well, he told me that they were dead. I kind of guessed that they were rich."

She looked down at her drink thoughtfully for a second or two, "My dad worked at a warehouse and my mom was a hotel maid. They made an ok living but when dad lost his job and mom got sick and was canned for missing too many days, we were in big trouble. Anyway, my dad was looking through the want ads one morning and Andy, who was, um, let's see, he had to be ten years old because we were just going into grade five..."

"You BOTH were going into grade five?"

She laughed, "D-uh! We're twins y'know!"

"You guys are twins?" I couldn't believe it.

She blushed a bit, "Not much of a family resemblance..." Then she brushed her hair back and said, "Well, as I was saying, dad was going through the paper and Andy picked up the financial section, you know where they print out all the stock reports? He pointed at this column and said, "Dremco Daddy! Dremco!" My dad just goes, "Yes son, that's a company on the New York Stock Exchange." Andy starts screaming, "Dremco! They'll make money! Lots of money!" I mean, he started throwing a real fit, pointing at the name Dremco and screaming and holy, I just remembered this now, he actually wet his pants!"

"Unbelievable." I said.

"Just wait! My mom comes in from the kitchen and sees Andy holding the paper and screaming and she's the kind who believes in everything from Tarot cards to tealeaves. So she kneels down in front of Andy and asks him why he's so excited and Andy sort of yells out that Dremco is going to make money. To make a long story short, she convinces dad to invest their savings in Dremco and in three days the company signs some kind of big deal contract and the stock soars."

"Holy."

"Yeah, but that's not it. After my parents made a nifty bundle they put Andy to the test and asked him to pick ten more companies out of the stock listing and he does."

"Every one a winner?"

"Every one."

"Wow."

She nodded, "I think it's the most marvellous thing in the world. I think it's a real gift from God. But Andy doesn't really think of it that way. I know that it can be a real burden for him."

You how I feel about stuff like that so you can probably picture my absent minded nod and how I changed the subject in lightning speed.

"I still can't believe you two are twins."

She laughed, "Yeah, but I'm not a seer. Not even a healer or anything." She took another sip of her drink, "I really got short changed in the whole gifts from above thing."

I let out a laugh, "Give me a break. Anyone can see…"

She looked at me expectantly and my voice sank down to a whisper, "I mean, you're so beautiful…"

She smiled weakly, probably because she was so used to everybody telling her how hot she was all the time. "Yeah, at first glance, it seems like I've got all the gifts, but it isn't the case."

"After a whole bunch of glances it's still pretty obvious." Holy, I was bold, must have been the booze. "Andy told me how you volunteer at the hospital and the senior's home AND the animal shelter."

She waved a dismissive hand. "I don't have to work so how else am I going to spend my days?" She smiled again. "Andy is the one with the true gifts though."

I shook my head slowly in wonder, "No doubt about that either. Your brother is pretty amazing. It's strange, that I've only known him a few days. It feels like I've known him, like, forever."

She leaned forward, "Yeah, isn't that strange? You guys act like you've been the best of friends for years." She paused, "It's almost magical."

The absent minded nod again, "It sure is."

There was a knock on the door and Cynthia got up to answer it. It was room service, wheeling in a tray with silver covers. I stood up and handed the guy a ten-dollar chip and he left with a smile towards my best friend's sister.

We pulled up two chairs and sat down across from each other. I was suddenly aware of my table manners so I ate slowly and carefully so as not to come across as a complete dork. The reason, you may have been asking yourself, is because I believed that something might actually happen between her and I. I was under that magical spell and there was a part of my foolish heart that believed that I was good enough for her.

She deftly popped a piece of toast into her mouth, "You and I have never talked either. I don't know a thing about you. Except that you're this guy that helped my brother out of a jam at the grocery store and ended up on a cross country trip."

I shrugged, "That's about all there is to know."

She shook her head, "That and you're a person who cares about people."

I laughed, "You really aren't psychic."

She said, with a look of sincerity aimed right into my eyes, "You care about Andy."

"I do. I really do and that's strange because it's not like me. Your brother is, well, he's my only friend." I grinned sheepishly, "Pathetic huh?"

She shook her head, "You're his only friend too."

"No, you're his friend."

She smiled sadly, "I'm his sister. I can try to be his friend along with his mother and babysitter and everything else but..."

I smiled as I cut her off, "Trust me, you're his friend too. Most sisters don't care. Mine don't anyway."

She poured a cup of tea for me, "See? I didn't even know you had sisters. C'mon, you can tell me your secrets, I'm not that much of a cow."

"I never thought that."

She laughed, "Yes you did."

I didn't know what to say so I just sipped my tea and mumbled, "Well, I don't think you are now."

She smiled, "Thank you. I don't think you're a free loading jerk anymore."

I held up my cup in a toast, "Thank you too."

"So tell on Macduff! Who is Zachary Kinfleisich?"

What is it about a beautiful person speaking your name? Isn't it almost musical? When she spoke it though, it was like looking into a mirror. I looked down at my plate and told her the truth, "A nobody. Really. There's nothing to tell."

She gave me a stern look that said that my self-deprecation wouldn't fly with her and she ate the last bit of egg on her plate and said with her mouth full, "I'll be the judge of that. What's your dad's name?"

"William."

"Good, now how about your mom?"

"Rita."

"Where did you go to school?"

"Bonaparte. How about you?"

"Oh no, we're not talking about me. What's your favourite sport?"

"Um, football I guess."

"Why, did you play?"

"Yup, for one season. Wide receiver. It's in my blood to run away from big guys."

She grinned, "What's your favourite food?"

"Spaghetti."

"Me too!"

"But we're not talking about you."

She laughed, "Ok, what's your favourite drink?"

"Ginger ale."

"Favourite fruit?"

"Oranges. Are my dietary preferences interesting?"

"Very. Favourite dessert?"

"Black forest cake."

"Yum." She looked up toward the ceiling. "Let's see, did I cover all the foods? Oh, what's your favourite nut?"

"The left one."

She burst out laughing, "Why? Does it have more character than the one on the right?"

I probably couldn't have come up with a witty retort to that but things were going in the right direction, talking about private parts and all. I think I was about to ask her if she had a breast preference but just then we could hear Andy outside in the hall, giggling with Cherisse. We were both dead silent as we listened to them fumble with the door and then enter the suite. The voices were barely a mumble even though we were killing ourselves trying to eavesdrop. After some walking around that lasted for a minute or so we could hear the bed give out a creak as two bodies crashed down on it.

Cynthia coughed nervously and then pushed her chair back and went over to the bed. She patted the quilt, "Ok, where were we?"

"We were just discussing..." Just then the bed next door gave another thunderous squeak and two voices began giggling.

"Sounds like they're having fun." I said, as the noise was so obvious and we both turned toward the wall like we expected to see plaster falling off.

"I hope she doesn't rob him in his sleep." She turned back to me, "You don't think she would do you?"

Why did she keep asking me these questions? As if I knew! Then I thought for a second or two and said, "What I really think is that she'll fall in love with him."

She smiled brightly, "Really?"

"Yeah, I mean, I think anyone that comes to know him also comes to love him."

"That's really sweet of you to say."

I leaned back against the wall and put my feet up on the bed, "It's the truth. A few days ago he was just another geek and now..."

"You love him too."

I smiled and pointed to the wall, "Well, not like Cherisse."

She smiled back, "I should hope not."

We sat gazing at each other and then she asked me a question that totally caught me off guard.

"Are you still lonely?"

I remembered Andy telling her that on the morning we left and I sighed, "The only friend I ever had was a guy named Tom Macgee." She didn't reply and I swallowed back a lump in my throat, because I tried to never think about him. "He died in grade ten. He was in a car accident."

I knew that Cynthia saw how difficult it was for me to utter that brief testimony and she ran her hand across my forehead, brushing the hair away. She whispered, "I'm so sorry." She bit her lip for a second and then said, "You don't have to feel lonely anymore."

I took a deep breath and decided to ruin the moment. Actually, it wasn't my intention to ruin the moment, that is, if there was going to be a moment, but something popped into my head and I had to get it out.

"Cynthia, is Andy really dying?"

I asked her, not because I didn't believe it, but because I didn't want to believe. It was brutal to have to look at Andy and think that there was a guy with a terminal disease. He was so full of life that death seemed like an impossibility.

She looked at me sadly and then lowered them to her lap. "Yes, he is."

I sighed, and closed my eyes.

"Arrhythmogenic right ventricular dysplasia."

"What?" I asked as I turned to look at her.

She gave a little shrug. "That's what he's got. And I dread every morning because I'm afraid that will be the day that he doesn't wake up."

I shuddered but didn't reply. I closed my eyes again, because honest to God, I felt like crying.

Suddenly, I felt her head on my lap and she let out a long sigh of her own. It wasn't a come on. It wasn't sexual at all but it's the closest thing to pure romantic love that I've ever felt. Yes, it even dwarfed all those childish feelings that I mistook for love and carried around from grade eight to grade twelve.

I ran my fingers through her hair and she put her hand on my lap and began to breathe softly. I kept stroking her hair and soon I could hear from her breathing that she had fallen asleep. I didn't mind, as it was so peaceful to just be near her and soon after I fell asleep too.

I'm sure I would have had the best dream of my life but I don't remember a thing because when I woke up the sun was already beginning its decent. We had slept the day away dressed in our fancy clothes and holding each other like frightened children. All of a sudden I could hear a tremendous ruckus going on next door with voices shouting and furniture being knocked around.

Cynthia was awake too and we both spent a few seconds looking at each other in dazed terror. "What's going on?"

I got up, "I don't know, but it doesn't sound good."

We both raced to the door and as soon as it was open I caught a sight of police uniforms and Andy being dragged out of the room in handcuffs.

"What the hell is going on here?" I yelled.

"Just get back in your room. This doesn't concern you." One of the cops said.

"Like hell I will. That's my brother!"

Upon hearing that, what I presumed to be the man in charge turned to me and said, "Your brother is coming with us."

There were four cops all engaged in subduing Andy, who was yelling and crying like a trapped animal. Cherisse stood in the doorway holding a sheet around her and looking quite terrified. The cops started to drag Andy toward the elevator and Cynthia and I were right on their heels, demanding answers and being ignored by the cops.

They got into the elevator and barred us from going in. Andy was yelling out to Cynthia and me and even screamed out to Cherisse, who hadn't budged from the doorway.

I said to Cynthia, "Go back to Cherisse and try to find out what the hell happened. I'm going to go after them."

Cynthia looked like she was going to go straight into a panic attack and with wide staring eyes she handed me the wrinkled tuxedo jacket that I had slept the day away in. "Please take care of Andy!"

I put the jacket on as I hit the elevator button furiously, "Don't worry, I will."

I realised that by the time the elevator would reach my floor Andy would be halfway to... wherever he was going. I looked over to the stairs and started off but Cynthia called out to me, "Zach, take care of yourself too!"

I waved to her and then crashed through the doors leading to the stairs. The first four flights were easy and my feet seemed to be running on air. The next ten went slower as I cursed cigarettes and my unused membership at the University health club. By the time I reached the lobby sweat was pouring off my face and I scared the hell out of the people who stood around the lobby checking in.

I burst through the big doors and looked up and down the strip but there was no police car, no flashing lights and no Andy. I stood there for only a second because I realised that the cops wouldn't have brought him out through the front, causing trouble for the hotel and the guests.

Making a quick choice, I opted to go left and half a block down was an alley, which I turned into blindly. Too fast, because not five feet in front of me was the police car, and before I had time to get out of the way I was jumping up onto the hood and rolling into the windshield, just like a Hollywood stunt man.

Thinking back, it probably looked really cool but at the time I was scared that I was going to die from a head on crash. Fortunately, the police car was only going about ten miles an hour and after a quick squeal of the brakes, I rolled off and was immediately accosted by a huge cop with a black moustache and a US Marines tattoo on his forearm.

Without thinking, I started to struggle and screamed out for them to let Andy go, that he hadn't done anything wrong and all cops were pigs. Not very wise, I know, but adrenaline has a way of putting words in your mouth.

I couldn't hear a word that was being said to me but I understood the backward chokehold and the feel of handcuffs being snapped on to my wrists.

I think the cops were trying to avoid a scene out in public so the burly former marine shoved me into the back of the patrol car in less than five seconds, "You're under arrest for obstructing an officer. Do you understand that?"

I nodded and he began to read me my rights as I struggled to get comfortable, because I seemed to be sitting on my thumbs.

"Quit squirming around back there!" The cop barked as he got back into the car. His partner in the driver seat looked up into the rear view mirror as he pulled out onto the strip, "What the hell is your problem buddy?"

"You just arrested my brother without any kind of explanation. I was trying to find out what was going on."

The big guy on the right said, "Sonny, we can arrest any criminal without stopping to give an explanation to you."

"Ok fine, I get that, but can you at least tell me what it was you busted him for?"

"Resisting arrest." The big guy said.

I couldn't believe it. "Resisting arrest? You arrested him for resisting arrest? That's like being killed by death."

The driver chuckled, "Killed by death. I like that."

The big guy turned in his seat, "Your brother was arrested for causing a disturbance and disorderly conduct in a public place. When we tried to talk to him he became verbally and physically abusive, hence the resisting arrest."

"Huh?"

"Listen pal, I already told you I don't have to explain anything to you. But you can be happy now, because you and your brother are going to be together real soon."

I turned back and saw another police car, presumably the one that held Andy, and I wondered how he was faring with his two legal abductors.

"Hey, do you usually send four guys to arrest someone for causing a disturbance?"

"Shut up." Burly Jar Head quipped.

I watched the strip melt away in the dusk and said to anyone who cared to listen, "This is great. Just great."

DAY SEVEN

Saturday the Sixteenth

Andy was booked and processed before me because the stupid ex marine, who probably got kicked out of the military for not knowing how to use a computer, couldn't get the computer to work. Consequently, by the time he took my fingerprints and snapped a cute little mug shot, Andy was already long gone, down a dingy hallway that led to the cells.

The cop looked at my driver's license, "I thought you said that guy was your brother."

I said, "Well, I'm engaged to his sister. We're sort of almost brothers in law." I really enjoyed telling that lie.

He nodded, "Ah, I see. Place your belongings in this tray."

I used my phone call trying to get a hold of Cynthia but the clerk at the hotel said she wasn't in her room. I asked him to ring up Andy's room but there was no answer. After my foiled attempt at calling in the cavalry I was led down the same hall that Andy had been taken. There was a row of empty cells and I was led to the one right at the very end, which held two people: Andy, and some old drunk.

As soon as the guard put me in Andy smiled and gave me a little wave but the drunk came to life, "Waiter, I'll have another gin and tonic."

I was all set to ignore him, seeing that he was bombed out of his tree but he yelled it out a second time, "Hey waiter! I said I'd have another gin and tonic!"

"Just ignore him," Andy said, "He said the same thing to me when I was brought in." He grinned, "Must be the tuxedos."

I noticed that we were still wearing matching monkey suits and I said, "I didn't think you would still be clothed after the way we left you."

He grinned, "I wasn't, but the cops were nice enough to let me put something on before they hauled me off."

He kept grinning, like he wanted me to ask him about the previous night so I forgot about our surroundings for the time being and said, "So, you and Cherisse get along ok?"

His grin grew even wider, "Sure did. Today I am a man."

"Here's to you then sonny!" The drunk yelled as he lifted an imaginary glass in a toast.

I smiled, "Get any sleep at all? You look like crap."

"No sleep at all!" He smoothed his hair out, "But I thought I would be glowing."

"OK, you look like glowing crap."

He laughed, "So what about you? Were you a gentleman with my sister?" His smile was as lewd as they come but I kept my face stony. "Yes. You see, my clothes are wrinkled because I slept in them, not because I tossed them off in breakneck speed."

He actually looked concerned, "Really? I would have sworn that you and she... y'know."

"I know!" The drunk bellowed.

"No," I said, "We just sat around and talked about you."

"Sheesh, bo-ring."

"No, it was nice actually."

He smiled, "Cherisse and I talked a lot too." He punched my arm, "I'm glad for you and Cynthia. Really."

"And I'll be glad for you if you tell me you used protection. I hate to thing what's all crawling around down there."

Andy gave me a hard look and I added with a friendly smile, "Because, y'know, I don't think Cherisse is the most, uh, virtuous…"

Andy got to his feet, "Don't talk about her like that. I'm serious now."

I sighed, "Oh Andy, wake up. She's no shrinking violet." I still have no idea what that phrase means, shrinking violet… but it sounded good at the time.

He stuck his finger into my chest, "She is NOT what you think she is!"

I wasn't about to get bullied by the guy that I had just thrown myself in front of a police car for, "And what is it that I think she is? A hooker? Or just another slut that goes for crisp twenties and casino chips?"

Andy answered with a wild right hand that connected with, what else, my nose. It wasn't a hard shot and it didn't bleed but it still stung. I held it gingerly while Andy looked poised to throw another one.

"Take it back!"

"Screw you." I mumbled while I held my nose.

He threw another one but I ducked and took a step backwards but he was right on top of me throwing a quick left that got me right in the stomach and then another right that got me smack on the lip.

I fell back, hitting my head on the wall and before I landed on my butt I yelled out, "SORRY! I'm sorry damn it!"

He stood over me, "Don't you ever, and I mean ever talk about her like that."

"Ok ok, just settle down Tyson."

He went back to the bench that he was sitting on and lit a cigarette. He puffed angrily, sending out clouds of blue smoke as he stared out at the bars. I looked down at my shirt and saw blood. My nose, as well as my lip began to bleed and I searched my pockets for a handkerchief.

The drunk saw my plight and held up an off white rag to me, "Here you go my young pugilist."

I sneered, "No thanks."

Andy said, "Why don't you take the handkerchief? Are you afraid it has the clap?"

"Oh shut up Andy, I apologized already."

The drunk put the rag back in his pocket and cleared his throat, "Since I am unable to offer you a good turn, perhaps you could do me a small favour?"

I looked up at him, "What?"

"Just a cigarette my finely attired sophisticate. Just to soothe my frazzled nerves and pounding head."

I took a cigarette out of my pack and before tossing one to him I said, "You don't sound too drunk now."

He smiled, "Merely a defence mechanism. Sometimes even hardened criminals show mercy to the town drunk. You see, this is not my first incarceration and for a recidivist like myself, I find that acting the part of the harmless inebriate is the safest part to play. If you two were the violent type then I would have continued the charade. You see there is nothing less threatening than an old intoxicated babbler."

I pointed to my nose, "This doesn't seem like the actions of a violent man?" I looked over to Andy who ignored my last comment.

The old man chuckled, "That was hardly worthy enough to be called a jailhouse brawl. Besides, it would seem that your violent demeanours are exclusive, not intended for those not, well, directly involved."

I rolled my eyes and tossed him the cigarette. He missed and scooped it off the floor without even brushing it off. "Thank you, thank you. You have a good heart and a soul bent on charity. Obviously I find myself in a cell with a true nobleman."

His manner of speaking put me off because there's nothing worse in my books than some pretentious drunk. Andy, on the other hand, seemed intrigued and was quick to walk over and offer the man a light.

"Ah, here is another man of high breeding! Thank you sir, thank you." He took a large drag and let the smoke curl out of his nostrils, "Now that is a right proper smoke that is."

Andy grinned, "They're Turkish!"

"Turkish? Ah my young dervish, you melt an old man's heart. I lack the words to fully express my gratitude, though if I could conjure them all, they would still do me shame."

Andy got into the spirit of things by bowing low, "Was it not said, "Men of few words are the best men.""

The old man's eyes lit up and he seemed tickled pink. "Yes it was, by Shakespeare! In Henry the Fifth, act three!" He levelled his merry eyes at Andy, "But here is a learned man before me!" He stood up and bowed to Andy, "Thou art a scholar; speak to it Horatio!"

Andy clapped his hands in supreme glee, "I love Shakespeare!"

The drunk beamed. "Then you and I should get along famously." He extended his hand to Andy, "Dr. Theodore S. Wainwright, professor of English Literature, UNLV."

Andy shook his hand, "A pleasure Dr. Wainwright. I'm Andrew Tiernan."

The old professor took his seat again and smiled. "It is an immeasurable pleasure to see a youngster who enjoys the immortal bard."

Andy sat down on his own bench, near the professor, "I think everyone should read Shakespeare. After all, he wrote for the common man!"

Theo lifted an eyebrow. "Did he?"

Andy looked a little stunned. "Of course! Those Elizabethan plays were what everyday people went to. That was their entertainment, their Saturday afternoon matinees!"

"Granted, but the common man could never appreciate the depth and beauty of Shakespeare. The author himself would never have intended it."

Andy sputtered, "He wouldn't have written all those plays to be enjoyed only by the elite."

"Ah, but those that understand and appreciate art ARE the elite. Be they rich or poor, free or slave. There are some who will never understand Shakespeare, just like they will never appreciate Bach, or see the beauty in the Mona Lisa, or grasp the concepts of Plato. You see Andrew, the common man..." He chuckled, "Is simply common."

"I disagree! I think everyone could enjoy all those things if they only tried."

"But what would be the point in trying? If one has to work at pleasure, then it ceases to be pleasurable."

Hi, me again. Normally I would drift off to sleep when two people start discussing art, culture and the like but those two really got on together and it was kind of neat to see them argue. It also showed me that Andy had a brain as well as a heart. Beyond that though, I wasn't too interested in what was being said so I entertained myself by watching two roaches fight over a crumb.

I just sat there, watching the little critters go at it but only a fraction of my brain was focused on them. The other ninety nine percent thought about Cynthia. How beautiful she was, the way her blue eyes would cast a reflection if you stared into them. Her nose was so cute and perfect. Her lips, full and red, demanding to be kissed. Her teeth, the one tooth on the left that was a little, just a little bit, crooked. The sophisticated high cheekbones and the swoop of her neck. I had to stop there because the rest of her was not to fit to think about in the company of other men.

I replayed all of our time together and even when she was being rude and nasty to me, I figured she was right in doing so. God, did I mention how beautiful she was? Did I ever mention how I would claw my way up to the peaks of Olympus and dethrone Venus with Cynthia's image? God, my legs ached from her sleeping on them but it was the most delicious pain and I never wanted it to leave. It was torture to be away from her when it seemed that I just found her. When we finally talked, smiled, joked and looked at each other. It was pure pain, a wholesome pain. My heart felt incomplete away from her.

I blinked away a tear, an actual tear! Then I cast a furtive glance over to my two cellmates to see if they had noticed. Theo the drunk was on his feet, his hands behind his back like he was giving a lecture. Andy was leaning forward with his elbows on his knees, listening closely.

"You see Andrew, Shakespeare never really gave life to his characters. He made talking mannequins!" He leaned close, "Do you see these wrinkles? Tell me how they came to be. What sorrows did I endure for me to be so scarred?"

Andy shook his head, "I don't know."

"Exactly! But you can imagine a thousand possibilities! Why was Antonio so sad? In sooth, he himself did not know and neither do we! Why is Iago such a villain, Richard such a devil? We're given hints, certainly, but we can guess and imagine and make wild suppositions about what happened before Act One, Scene One! Do you see Andrew? Every writer, playwright and storyteller must make bottomless pits in the hearts of their characters! We can never be told the whole story and we don't want to be! We have to be a part of its creation!"

Meanwhile, cockroach number one, whom I had named Felix, had utterly defeated his arch nemesis, Tom. Tom of the droopy antennae, the brave but vanquished warrior of Cell Block C.

The two of them, meaning Andy and the professor, went at it for another hour while I leaned back and smoked, wondering how the hell we were going to get out of jail and what the hell had happened that landed us in this fix.

I cleared my throat, "Sorry to interrupt you two, but I was just wondering..."

Andy sneered, "Screw off. I'm not talking to you."

"Could you at least tell me why the hell you got arrested in the first place?"

"No, because that would mean talking to you."

"Well you're talking to me now!"

"Oh yes, so I am." With that he turned back to Theo the drunk.

I kicked the bars in frustration and that brought a yell from one of the cops. "Shut up in there! If there's any kicking going on it's going to come from my boot!"

I know I shouldn't have, but I did, "Yeah, you and who else?"

The boots came our way and all three of us tensed for a prison scene beating.

The cop who had arrested Andy came over and stood with his fists on his hips, "Who said that?"

Silence.

He asked again in low and menacing voice, "Who said it?"

Before I could admit to it the cop turned to Andy, "Was it you? You little bastard, I should drag you out here and wipe my ass with your face!" He went right up to the bars, "You screw my wife and now you tell me off? I've got news for you dick head, if you think you're gonna walk out of here on your own two feet you got another thing coming. So shut the hell up if you don't want to endure the beating of your life!"

A firm voice from down the hall yelled out, "Charlie! You leave those prisoners alone!"

Charlie snorted a nose full of snot and spat in Andy's direction. "Just teaching these criminals a thing or two about Las Vegas courtesy!"

He stomped off in the direction that he had come and as soon as he was out of earshot I whispered savagely at Andy, "What did he mean about his wife? Is that Cherisse's husband?"

He whispered back, "EX husband."

I covered my eyes, "Oh man. You sure can pick em Andy."

He looked at me with his upper lip curled into a sneer, "Yeah, I sure can."

I stood up, "And what the hell is that supposed to mean? I'm in here because I tried to save your ass!"

He smiled sarcastically, "Well you sure did a helluva job!"

I was ready to throw a few punches of my own but Theo stood up between us, "Now now boys, please, we can deal with each other with some civility if we're going to be cellmates."

Just then another cop came striding down the hall and opened the door. "OK Theo, you can go now. Just try to lay off the booze ok?"

"Officer, you are a true gentleman with the soul of a poet. I hope that I will not inconvenience you in the future and it is my deepest hope…"

"Yeah yeah, save the speeches for the students."

Theo paused at the door, "Andrew, it was a true pleasure and I wish you the best! And you, my young friend whose name I never did catch, I also wish you a pleasant and prosperous future!"

Andy gave him a courteous wave and I nodded to him as he was led away.

Andy looked away and sat back down on the bench, lighting up another cigarette and blowing the smoke towards the ceiling.

"So this Charlie guy busts you just because you slept with Cherisse?"

"Shut up."

"C'mon Andy, how many times do you want me to apologize? Man, I don't even know why the hell I AM apologizing. I'm in this rat hole because..."

He finally broke, "I know, and I'm sorry too." He came over with his hand extended, "Friends again?"

I shook his hand, "Friends. Now can you please tell me what happened?"

He sat down next to me, "I guess some friend of Charlie's spotted me with Cherisse and told him. He found out where I was staying and busted in with some bogus disturbing the peace charge. I was livid because Cherisse had told me all about Charlie and how he was completely nuts and totally jealous. That's why she left him in the first place. None of this was her fault and she's not the girl you think she is. Really, she's sweet."

I lay my head back against the wall. "Well, we're in for it now; whatever the reason is."

He put his head back, "Cynthia will get us out. Cherisse too."

"I hope so Andy, I really do."

After a few minutes of silence Andy tapped my leg, "So nothing happened with you and Cynthia?"

I opened my eyes, "Well, I wouldn't say nothing happened."

"Uh huh, go on."

"Nah, nothing like that. We talked, but it was really nice."

"Y'know, I had a feeling about you two. Remember how I said you were the one who was going to tame the shrew?"

I grinned, "Common people like you shouldn't quote Shakespeare."

He laughed, "But I'm not common!"

I smiled, "No, that's true. Common is something you definitely are not."

He wiped some dirt off the knee of his pants, "I'm happy for you guys."

"Don't get carried away. I told you nothing really exciting happened. I don't even know if she likes me."

He laughed, "You ARE stupid."

"Another reason why she couldn't like me."

He leaned forward and looked me straight in the eye, "Do you like her?"

"Yeah, but what I feel has nothing to do with..."

"When did you start liking her? A couple days ago you said she had the personality of a troll. Is it just her looks that you like?"

"No! I... ah Andy..." I looked at him shrewdly, "I don't remember ever telling you she had the personality of a troll."

"Well, you thought it."

"I hate this psychic crap!"

He grinned, "Don't change the subject. Is it just her looks that you like?"

"I don't want to talk about it."

"Yes you do. When did you start liking her?"

I didn't hesitate because I knew right away. "After the fight in the parking lot."

"That's when she started liking you too."

That sent a jolt up my spine, "Did she tell you that?"

He smiled, "She didn't have to. I'm psychic remember?"

"Ok then Kreskin, so what's in store for us? Marriage? A long and happy life with 2.5 kids?"

"2.5 kids?" He shuddered. "I sincerely hope that you don't end up having half a kid."

"Seriously."

He shook his head. "I don't know and you don't want to know. Otherwise, where's the fun, the excitement?"

I narrowed my eyes at him. "I really don't like you psychics."

"Well," He said, "We like you just fine."

"So Mesmo the Magnificent, when do we get out of here?"

He looked at his watch, "Now."

"What do you mean now?"

Another jolt went up my spine but it didn't feel anything like the excitement of Cynthia liking me. That jolt was bliss; the other one freaked me out, because just then footsteps could be heard coming down the hall.

I stared at Andy with an open mouth and he winked at me. The little jerk actually winked at me.

The guard who had let Theo out stuck a key in the lock and swung the door open, "OK boys, your time is up."
"What do you mean up?" I asked.
"Charges were thrown out. You're free to go."
I was curious as hell but I wasn't going to ask any more questions so I picked up my jacket that I had been using as a pillow and was out the door in a flash. Cherisse's ex husband was nowhere in sight and in the reception area the guard gave me back all the junk in my pockets which included my wallet, change and eight thousand dollars in casino chips.
I looked around but couldn't see any sign of Cynthia, who I figured had used her gift of bitchiness to get the charges dropped. I was almost foaming at the mouth to see her and when Andy was through I had him by the arm, dragging him out the door.

Right on the curb, in the glow of the streetlight stood an angel and next to her was Cherisse, and standing behind the both of them was Bobby Fabian, smiling through the cigarette that was clenched between his teeth. As soon as Cherisse saw Andy, she was racing up the police station steps to give him a rib-crushing hug and kiss. I don't know how little Andy did it, but he lifted her up as they kissed and even though they didn't seem to mind, I looked away so as not to be rude.

I left them on the third step as I slowly walked down to the curb. I felt shy as I smiled and great God in Heaven Who I tried not to believe in, Cynthia smiled too; a tiny smile that looked like it was going to burst out into a laugh.
I stopped in front of her and said, "How did you..."

Just like her brother, she had a habit of interrupting people but I liked the way she did it a lot better. She put her arms around me and kissed me, fully, passionately, heavenly, right on the lips. I didn't try to lift her up and swing her around the way Andy did but I did kiss her back. I put my arms around her waist and drew her close, so close, to me. I didn't even wonder if I was a good kisser, if she liked it, or whether my breath was ok. It was a kiss where the only thinking going on takes place in the heart. And what thoughts my little heart was churning!

The kiss lasted a long time but not nearly long enough. When we parted, hands lingering on hips, we smiled shy smiles again. Then, either to break any forthcoming tension or just because a passionate kiss releases such joy, we laughed. We looked up at Andy and Cherisse, who had also exchanged their kiss for a desperately beautiful embrace. Andy, whose head rested against Cherisse's shoulder, opened his eyes and smiled at us. Then he kissed Cherisse on the cheek and the two of them came down the steps holding hands.

Bobby gave me a poke in the ribs, "Good to see you kid, hope you got through your prison term without being anybody's girlfriend."

I smiled, sincerely. That's how happy I felt.

Andy came down the stairs with a wide grin, "Hey Bobby! I didn't expect to see you again!"

"Are you kidding? Once I heard you got busted I was frantic! Knowing that my newest and bestest buddy was behind bars was enough to give me a heart attack!"

Andy laughed and clapped me on the back, "Didn't I tell you the girls would get us out?"

I smiled at Cynthia, "Never had a doubt."

Cherisse said, "OK gang, a bite to eat before you breeze out of town?"

"I could sure use something to eat but are we leaving already? I was looking forward to another long bath at the hotel."

Cynthia shook her head, "Sorry babe, the conditions of your release are that we get out of Dodge without going within ten feet of a casino."

Andy laughed, "That figures! A good night at the tables and everyone panics. They're afraid that if I spend another night in town I'll end up owning it."

Cherisse laughed, "Are they wrong?"

Andy gave her a quick kiss on the cheek, "No, they're not."

Cynthia took the car keys out of her purse and led us to the Mercedes, which needed a wash almost as badly as Andy and I. Andy wiped his hands on his pants, "Man, I need a shower." He paused and looked at me, "Almost as bad as you do."

I gave him a big hug, which made him squirm. "Oh Andy, don't you like my au-naturel scent?"

I wouldn't let go and he struggled to get out of my grip, "No! You smell like a sewer!"

The girls and Bobby were laughing and soon Andy joined in too. I let him go and Cynthia came over to me with a smile, "I don't mind it. It's a masculine smell."

Andy corrected her, "You mean bestial."

I opened my arms to give him another hug and he backed off, "Just kidding!"

We drove to a family style restaurant on the outskirts of town and we all had flapjacks with maple syrup. Crowded together in a corner booth, we had a toned down food fight and it wasn't long before we all were covered in Aunt Jemima stickiness; giggling and laughing like high school kids skipping school. We all wore goofy smiles and we laughed at any stupid little thing. It was freedom and a moment torn out of the pages of Time, to be read and reread with reverence.

Cherisse seemed like a different person. She even looked different to me. Her clothes, instead of looking sluttish, seemed only complimentary and sexy. Her demeanour was still brash but it was spirited, not cheap.

I turned to her during the meal and said, "So how did you two pull it off?"

She smiled, "Cynthia threatened to sue the entire police department."

Andy and I laughed but Cynthia waved her hand, "But it wouldn't have done any good at all if not for Cherisse. She had a little talk with Charlie and put the fear of God into him."

"Actually," Cherisse said with a wry smile, "I put the fear of my divorce lawyer into him. I told him that I would cut off his visitation rights if he didn't drop the charges."

"Visitation rights?" I asked, like having children was too much of a grown up concept to be applied to one of the high school kids in our quintet.

Andy grinned, "You bet. Cherisse has a daughter." He put his arm around her, "And little Andrea is going to grow up to be as beautiful as her mother."

Bobby nodded, "A sweet little angel that Andrea is."

Cherisse narrowed her eyes at him, "You've never even met her."

"I don't have to see her to know she's an angel! She's YOUR daughter and YOU'RE an angel!"

Cherisse let out a loud guffaw and Bobby feigned a hurt look, "Cherisse honey, if there's one thing I know, its angels!" He stood up, banged his fork on the table a few times and began a loud, extremely off key version of "Dream Angel."

Andy clapped, "Go man go!"

Cynthia buried her face on my shoulder while I laughed and whistled for more.

Cherisse tugged on the hem of Bobby's coat, "Bobby sit down! You're so awful!"

He did stop, and with another hurt look he said, "What do you mean I'm awful? An awful singer doesn't go on Middle Eastern tours and pack Vegas ballrooms!"

We all laughed and I said, "Hey Bobby, were you really in the middle east?"

He nodded resolutely, "Damn right! I was in Vermont for two months!"

"That's New England!" Andy laughed.

"England, Middle East, they're all foreign countries!" He sat back down, "And if you don't think Vermont is like a foreign country you should go there! They're animals! Complete rubes!" He took a large sip of his drink, "They're not like us at all!"

Cynthia snickered, "I'm sure they're all very grateful."

"Hey, you can laugh if you want," Bobby said with a straight face, "But for a guy with absolutely no talent to make a living as a singer for the past seventeen years is no small feat, let me tell you."

Andy leaned over and gave him a hug around the shoulders, "Bobby, you've got loads of talent! You're the greatest singer I've ever heard!" He lifted his glass, "C'mon guys, hoist 'em for the greatest Bobby Darin impersonator in the world!"

Bobby clinked his glass against his, "Don't forget Fabian!"

"Fabian too!" We all yelled.

The waitress, who had been casting worried looks our way all evening long finally came by, "I'm really sorry, but I have to ask you guys to keep it down."

Andy said, "I'm sorry." He put down a Fifty Dollar bill, "For you dearest, for being the best waitress in all of Las Vegas."

Cherisse punched his arm, "Hey!"

Andy cringed, "Oh, but you're not a waitress anymore! You're a student! The best nursing student ever! C'mon guys, hoist 'em again for the best nursing student in the world!"

We all lifted our glasses again. I smiled, "Nice recovery buddy!"

We laughed, drank and munched on stale desserts for another hour and then Bobby leaned back and said, "Well kids, it's time for this codger to get to work. I can't let the fans at the Ozone down."

He leaned over and shook my hand, "Zach, it was a pleasure. Next time you're in town, don't forget to see my show and burp along to Mack the Knife."

I smiled, "Be good Bobby, it was great meeting you."

He turned to Cynthia and kissed her hand, "Cynthia, if it wasn't for this young buck to your left, I would have pursued you to the ends of the earth."

Cynthia smiled sweetly, "You would have had to."

Bobby grabbed his chest, "Ouch!" Then he added, "A few more hours with me and you would have changed your mind."

Sweet smile in place, "A few more hours with you and I..."

Andy cut her off, "Enough! That's no way for parting friends to act."

Bobby turned to him and gave him a bear hug, knocking over two water glasses with his elbow. "Andy, you are the livin' end and I kid you not! I haven't met a character like you in... Ever! You gotta promise me to come back real soon!"

I don't think Bobby noticed, but Andy's face had a flash of pure sadness that almost brought tears to my eyes. He nodded, "I will."

It was at that point that I had a morbid thought burst into my brain. Namely, that Andy didn't intend on coming back. Los Angeles would be the last stop on our trip and in his life.

Cherisse put her hand to Andy's cheek, "I'm going to get going too lover. I'll see you on your way back from L.A."

Andy nodded, "You know it."

He said it very quickly, with just a hint of sadness and regret. I imagine that he had been practising the good-bye in his mind since he had met her. Cynthia reached under the table and squeezed my hand and when I looked over to her she had tears in her eyes. She quickly brushed them away and put on a strained smile.

Andy kissed Cherisse. "I'll walk you to the car, love."

She smiled, "Of course, I can't give you a proper farewell with all these people watching."

We all stood up and Cherisse came over to Cynthia and me. She embraced Cynthia and then me. Her lips were close to my ear and she whispered, "Bring him back to me safe and sound. I'm counting on you Zach."

I nodded, but only said, "I'll see you soon. Take care."

They put their coats on and we all gave little waves while Andy led them out. He called to us over his shoulder, "I'll be right back."

Cynthia sat down and let out a sigh, "It just isn't fair. Just when he falls in love he has to..." Her words trailed off as she stifled a sob.

I put my arm around her, "I know, it doesn't seem right."

She dabbed at her eyes with the napkin, "I can't let Andy see me cry. He made me promise so many times that I wouldn't."

I shook my head, "I feel like crying myself, even though..." I looked away quickly.

"Even though what?"

I turned back to her, looking into her glittering eyes, "Even though I feel so happy being with you."

She let a tear come as she kissed me softly, "I'm happy too. I really am." She ran her hand down my cheek to my chin and cupped it, "Andy wants us to be happy together. I feel it."

I nodded, smiling, "I feel it too."

She sighed. "It's really horrible for Cherisse though. At least she's taken care of, financially anyway. She told me that Andy gave her all the money that he won last night."

I whistled, "That's a nice gift."

"She's been planning on going to school for years but she had to take care of Andrea."

I said, "I really had her pegged wrong though. When I first saw her I thought... well, you know."

"I know; I felt the same way. I spent the whole day with her and all she could talk about was Andy. She admitted that the money was the motivator at first; after all, she's a single mother with a daughter to raise and in this town, that's the only way to live. But then she said, and get this, that Andy was magic. He made her feel things that were out of this world. Magic, just like you said."

I nodded, "He is magic."

"She said she wanted to move to Edmonton, she wanted to be with Andy."

I was about to ask her if she thought that Andy would live past L.A but just as I was about to speak she motioned to the door with her chin; "Here he comes."

Andy walked stiffly, like he was bearing a huge burden but didn't want anyone to know it. His shiny, happy eyes were red from shedding tears. He came over to the table and said in a voice just barely above a whisper, "Let's go see the ocean."

DAY EIGHT

Sunday the Eighteenth

There was no singing along to the radio when we left Las Vegas shimmering in the desert behind us. There were no travelling games and no idle chatter; only the low grumble of the engine and three minds bent on death.

Andy drove and I sat next to him, flicking looks over to him every few minutes. He looked terrible. There were huge bags that had mysteriously appeared under his eyes and the three days without sleep had finally caught up to him and dug sharp claws deep into his chest. He was having difficulty breathing and he looked even more pale than usual. He didn't seem to notice my constant looks as he kept his eyes focused on the road ahead. Cynthia leaned back and stuck her leg between the seat and the door so I could touch her, and somehow fight off the loneliness that hung over us.

We didn't travel far, as exhaustion finally took its toll on Andy. We pulled into a Super Eight within sight of San Bernardino and Andy let out a long breath and slumped over the steering wheel. I was the one who went in to get the rooms and took the same one as Andy so he wouldn't be alone. I held Cynthia's hand outside her room. "I'm staying with Andy."

She smiled sadly and kissed my cheek. "That's sweet of you." She whispered.

I looked down at my feet and it felt like a crack went through my heart. "He's going to die, Cynth."

She lifted my chin and looked me dead in the eye. "It seems like every day I wake up and that's the first thing I think of. I remember that he has a terminal disease and this could be his last day on earth. Whenever I feel like that knowledge will tear me apart, Andy reminds me that everyday could be everyone's last day. He tells me that life is for living and he reminds me to grab hold of life every single day." She sighed, "It wasn't until I met you that I began to do it. Do you know that you're the reason…" She waved a hand in front of her face, as if to erase her words. Then she smiled, "Go with Andy and be happy… be happy for him."

"I'll try." I said, and then we kissed, long and gently.

I spent the night on my side; facing Andy's curled up form on the bed next to mine. His breathing was shallow and laboured, his body moving only when he let out a sob. My trying to be happy for him lasted all of ten seconds and from then on, I was biting my lip and feeling my heart break. I felt like I was sitting on the moon and watching the world die in front of me. It must have been around three, when that same moon sent bright, borrowed light into the room. Andy turned over and lay there, staring right into my eyes.

We stared at each other for a long time and I don't remember having even a single clear thought during that time. It was Andy who blinked once, slowly, and then said in a whisper, "Don't worry. Just go to sleep."

I looked at him for another minute or so until I closed my eyes and took deep breaths waiting for sleep. I only woke up once after that and when I opened my eyes I saw Andy wasn't in bed. He was at the desk, scribbling on motel stationary and humming a song under the soft light of the desk lamp. I fell right back to sleep and didn't have a single dream.

When I woke up Andy was making his bed and singing "Dream Lover." I yawned and he smiled, "Morning Zachary."

"Morning." I mumbled as I rubbed my eyes.

"Hey man," he said, "I want you to forget about last night if you can. Push the bad aside and look at my big smile and then copy it."

I didn't know what he was saying and the look I gave him told him just that.

"What I mean is," He started fluffing the pillow as he spoke. "Don't be depressed, because I'm not. OK?"

I nodded, "Ok Andy, you got it."

He smiled, and I tried to as well, but I could feel my lips stretch in one of those smile attempts that look hideous.

Of course he saw it but was unsure what to do. I was, after all, sad because of him. He wanted me to bury pity, compassion and all those other noble emotions that I wasn't even feeling. What I felt was a selfish sadness, because he would be gone from my life and it seemed that everything good that I had felt a hundred miles ago would be gone. I grabbed my stuff and went into the bathroom but I didn't shower right away. Once again, I stared hard into the mirror and I was actually surprised at just how depressing my reflection looked.

I guess I had never really been happy. In my shallow life, pleasure was a substitute for happiness. Something good happens and then I'm happy. Two seconds later something bad happens and then I'm pissed off or depressed or just sitting around watching TV and not thinking. Being around Andy meant that I did think and I did feel but no matter how much he wanted me to be happy, I couldn't.

Las Vegas was miles behind us, and the "big thing" that Andy had anticipated came and went. Just like my whole damn life. Beyond a cheerful Christmas before my dad ran off, or a birthday party where some kids actually showed up, I wasn't happy. Andy had me pegged from day one, when I overheard him tell Cynthia that I was just lonely. Lonely, sad and pathetic, what a great resume I had.

But I was in love with a gorgeous woman and in love, in a different sense, with her brother. It wouldn't last, because for me, all good things end. I stood there in that stinking bathroom, depressed to beat hell and yearning, absolutely yearning for joy. Away from home, from real life, from all fears and insecurities and little worries meant that I was free, and I wasted my freedom by feeling terrible.

After my shower the three of us had our breakfast and I could feel Cynthia watching me expectantly as I poked the fork around my eggs. Andy seemed cheerful, talking about LA and listing off the things we could do once we arrived, but there was no conviction in his voice. He and Cynthia exchanged a few looks and then he announced that he was going to get the car washed and gassed up.

Cynthia grabbed my hand suddenly and leaned close to me, "What's wrong?"

I sighed, "You know what's wrong. It's Andy."

"Andy's fine, he's in high spirits. He's really looking forward to LA."

"And what about after LA? What happens to him after that?" I took out a cigarette but I paused before lighting it. I mumbled something and Cynthia said, "What did you say?"

I shrugged, "Nothing."

In case you're curious, I said, "What happens to us?"

I didn't repeat it because I already knew the answer. Cynthia and I would only be two people with fond memories. Without Andy, we were through, and that was enough to keep me sinking fast in my own slough of despondency. She must have heard me anyway. "We go on Zach, that's what happens after LA." She reached out and took my hand, "Simple as that."

She looked so sincere that in that moment I believed her. We smiled, and I gave her hand a squeeze. When she looked out into the street I could feel myself slipping right back into the muck of reality.

Andy was the cement in our love and without him that love would crumble. He was the catalyst, the impetus behind our joining. Cynthia loved me when I came to Andy's rescue and I loved her when she came to mine. What would our love be without Andy? It would only be another damnable memory.

We paid the bill and sat outside on the curb, holding hands and searching for more words. We both took in little breaths like we were about to say something that would nail down all the feelings we had but we came up short each time and when Andy came back, she seemed as relieved as I was.

I got behind the wheel because Andy said he wanted to look at the scenery. I drove slowly hugging the right shoulder and watching the same scenery roll by in the morning sun. My depression spread and all of us knew that things were drawing to a close. We were silent and thoughtful as California drifted by.

"Andy's gonna die!" I wanted to scream to break the sorrow with anger. He would leave us, alone, forever, and the magic that he had spun in my life and in our love would pass away.

"Andy's gonna die." I wanted to whimper to quell the anger with true heartfelt regret. It was a pale sun kind of foreboding. A feeling warm, sticky and sad; like calling a happy dream to mind and knowing that it will never repeat itself or worse yet, ever come true. It's like Andy said to us a thousand miles back when he was in a philosophical mood, "The worst nightmares are the good dreams because we wake up and realise that it was all a lie."

Every bump in the road, every signpost and all things that the sunlight touched were more memories that would be gone forever. Like I keep reminding you, I'm limited by my shortcomings as a writer so I urge you to think of some painful memory from your own past to relate to how I felt. Remember when your dog died? How about the first time some person you loved treated you like dirt? Remember the first day of kindergarten when your mom left you alone for the first time? Are you thinking of those things? Good, because that's how depressed I felt.

I had to speed up to pass the bonehead in front of us who must have been looking for a good radio station and had to take his foot off the gas to do it. Just as the car edged over fifty, it let out a loud grumble and then shuddered like it caught a chill. After a couple unleaded hiccups it stalled. "Damn it." I said as I looked down at the quickly sinking speedometer needle.

"What happened?" Andy asked, leaning over to look at the instrument panel.

"No idea, it just died."

I steered over to the shoulder and turned the key off. Andy kept looking over at the dashboard, "This is odd."

We all sat there for about a minute, looking at the dashboard and waiting for a divine sign from the Mercedes god.

Cynthia was the first to offer any kind of wisdom, "Well, it's not doing us any good just sitting here." She opened her door a crack, turning back to make sure there weren't any cars coming, and then got out of the car.

Andy shrugged and got out on the passenger side and without bothering to check to see if it was clear, I opened the door and stepped out. A pickup truck narrowly missed me and the girl in the passenger seat stuck her middle finger out. I just shook my head and went around to the front of the car. I popped the hood and the three of us stood there looking down at the engine with looks of complete ignorance on our faces. "Think it might be the carburetor?" Cynthia asked.

"It's fuel injected." Andy said wisely enough.

"Think it might be the fuel injector?" Cynthia asked without a pause.

"Dunno." Andy sighed.

I pointed to a series of hoses, "Maybe it's that."

"That's the air conditioning." Andy said.

Cynthia took a step back, "What is it then, since you know so much."

Andy grinned, still looking down at the engine, "I don't know."

"That's just great." I said.

Andy turned around and faced us, still grinning, "This is a sign."

"What kind of sign?" Cynthia asked.

"Remember how I said that something big was going to happen in Las Vegas?"

We nodded.

"And something big did happen didn't it?"

Cynthia blushed and I let a little smile slip through.

"Well," Andy said with a rapidly expanding smile, "That big thing is tiny compared to what's waiting for us in Los Angeles!"

"What's going to happen?" I asked, now a true believer.

"I don't know! Something BIG!" Andy turned toward the steady stream of traffic and squinted. His voice went down to what sounded like a whisper against the noise of the cars going by, "Yup. Something big."

Cynthia and I both looked toward the road for the big thing to happen but the cars kept going by in a steady stream. I was the first to turn my attention back to the engine and a few minutes later Cynthia was beside me, sitting on the front bumper. Andy remained at the side of the road, staring at each passing car with an expectant look. Cynthia leaned forward, resting her elbows on her knees and looking at her brother. I shot a glance over to Andy and said quietly, "Any sign of a big thing coming?"

Cynthia shook her head, "Nope."

I took off the air cleaner and looked around the engine. Not that I had a clue about anything but it seemed more productive than just sitting around. I let out the odd mumble as I tinkered around and Cynthia swivelled toward me and said, "How many years have you been in University?"

"This fall it'll be 3 years."

She smirked, "All that book learnin' and you still don't know how to fix a car."

I smiled, "I'm a product of a liberal education. If we ever find ourselves in a situation where our lives depend on knowing a line from the Iliad, I'll have it covered."

She looked back to the road, "Yeah, that kind of thing happens all the time."

I poked my finger around the fuel injector, "You never know."

I noticed that one of the little fuel injector thingies was stuck and I said, "Hey, I think this little fuel injector thingie is..."

but I didn't get a chance to finish because all of sudden Cynthia was on her feet and tugging on my sleeve, "Someone's stopping!"

Pulling ahead of us on the shoulder was a matching black Mercedes, an exact copy, to be exact. Except what climbed out of the car to meet Andy wasn't a copy of any of us, except maybe Cynthia. A male Cynthia, if you get my drift. If you don't, I mean that this guy was really good looking. Drop dead good looking. Movie star good looking. Insane jealousy inspiring good looking. Don't get me wrong, it's not like I look at other guys and notice how attractive they are. I couldn't help it with this joker, because he was one of the exceptions.

The exceptions are the people that can get anything they want based solely on their looks. They don't have to be smart or funny or have any virtues to get ahead. All they have to do is look the way they do.

Let me tell you why I hated him before he even opened his mouth. The cut of his expensive clothes showed that lurking underneath was a body crafted by four nights a week at the gym and nothing less than perfect genes. He was a little shorter than I, with blonde hair that flowed in the wind like a scene in a movie. He walked with that smooth confidence that says, "Hi there ugly people, I hope you appreciate the fact that I'm strolling along in front of your unworthy eyes." He was a jerk without speaking and when he did speak, he became a pompous jerk.

"Having some car trouble?"

No dumb ass, we're parked on the side of the road with the hood up to give the engine a tan. (I didn't actually say it, but I thought it really loud so Andy could appreciate my wit).

Without any delay, he brushed past me and looked under the hood. He hummed as he poked around and less than a minute later he looked over his shoulder to me and said, "Go and see if she'll start."

I obeyed; because that's what the average do when told to do something by one of the beauties. You have no idea how much I wanted that engine to be dead but of course it roared to life and the first thing I saw when two tanned hands closed the hood of the car was this row of perfect white teeth smiling at me. Jerk.

If there was any justice at all in the world he would have a terrible case of psoriasis from the neck down but I knew that it was too much to hope for. Things never even out. Sure, there's a bunch of smart people who are ugly. There are tons of fat people with great personalities. But why are there good-looking smart people who have it all? A religious man would smile and say that God is not without mercy but I would answer that God may be merciful and loving, but He sure isn't fair.

I got out of the car and Andy was all smiles, shaking the stranger's hand and thanking him profusely. Cynthia looked awestruck, staring at tall, blonde and handsome with nothing less than wonder. I could feel my heart slowly hardening like clay left out in the sun and it wouldn't be the last time that day where I felt disused and pathetic.

"Philip Donasco." The blonde Adonis said as he stuck his hand out to me.
My first impulse was to turn around and walk away from him but where the hell was I going to go? I shook his hand, "Zach."
He shook Andy's hand as my little friend burst out his name, rank and serial number with such enthusiasm that I wanted to smack him. As Philip turned to Cynthia I resisted the urge to leap in between the two of them to shield my lover's eyes from the radiance. I stayed put, scowling as Philip Perfection smiled warmly, politely, in a way that was such a subtle, classy come on that I was near nausea with loathing and dread.

It wasn't my imagination, because reality is crueller than fiction; I swore that Cynthia gave him a smile equal in class, subtlety and politeness. It was a total come on smile. Not brazen enough to scare, not lewd enough to offend. A perfect movie scene smile that takes place before the hero and heroine join forces, save the world, kill the villain and hop into the sack.

Cynthia's voice sounded deeper and richer than normal. "Thank you so much Philip, we would have been stuck out here for hours if you hadn't stopped."

He smiled modestly, "It was nothing really. One of the fuel injectors just needed a little loosening."

I knew it! We wouldn't have been stuck for hours. It would have been mere minutes and I would have been the hero! Not this Perfect Bodied Boob that stood there smiling his fake modest smile. Did that sound bitter? I sure as hell hope so.

"Well, you saved us, and I owe you one." Andy smiled jubilantly.

"No problem at all." Philip said with a toothy smile.

I wanted to clap my hands together like my father used to do when the rest of the family was taking too long getting ready for our camping trips. "OK Campers, let's get to campin'!" He would say with enthusiasm and impatience. "Let's get at it while the gettin's good, let's stoke the fires, hit the road, get a move on, take off. C'mon Campers, let's get to campin'!"

We couldn't stay on that road with Philip. Bad things would happen. I could feel it. Maybe I was getting psychic myself. If we stayed and talked to the devil in J Crew, Andy would find a new best friend and my Cynthia was bound to fall in love and toss me aside like a piece of garbage. It was inevitable. I knew it. I just knew it.

"OK Campers!" I clapped my hands together and the three of them looked over at me. "Let's... get... to... uh..." I cleared my throat, "Maybe we should get going." I smiled, "Philip, thanks a lot man. Really, thanks." I walked over to him with my hand outstretched, "Thanks. Thanks so much." I swear you never saw a better example of a blithering idiot.

He shook my hand but Andy was being a very naughty camper. "Philip, you have to let me pay you back. I can't leave any outstanding debts."

Philip held his hand up, palm out. "No Andrew, you don't owe me. I'm just glad I could help."

Cynthia placed her hand on Philip's arm and smiled, "Please, there must be some way for us to repay you." She laughed, "You don't know my brother, he won't quit until you give in."

Philip laughed and said... how the hell do I know what that bastard said? In case you missed it, Cynthia placed her hand on his arm.

CYNTHIA PLACED HER HAND ON HIS ARM!

It took her, what, three days to say a nice thing to me, let alone touch my arm! At that rate she would be necking with him in two minutes! I was the one who got my nose bloodied not once, but twice for her little snot of a brother! What did jack off Blondie do? Get a little grease on his index finger while he loosened a thingamajig that I was just about to loosen in three seconds if he hadn't roared up in his Mercedes with his ivory smile and ebony hued, manufactured Gold's Gym body. How the hell do I know what he said?

"That sounds like a brilliant idea Philip." Andy said.

"Are you sure Philip? We're the ones who owe you." Cynthia said through her unwavering smile.

"It would be my pleasure." Philip said.

"What?" I moaned.

"Are you sure it isn't too much of an inconvenience?" Cynthia continued to croon.

"Not at all." Philip smiled back. "Besides, and I hope you don't get the wrong idea or anything, but I've got a feeling about you three. I just felt that I had to stop and lend a hand."

"What?" I asked.

"Absolutely brilliant." Andy said, "We'll follow you."

"I'll take it slow." Philip said as he backed toward his car, "The traffic in this town can be pretty harrowing."

"What?" I looked from Andy to Cynthia but a car had just roared by and they didn't hear me.

Philip got into his car and Cynthia skipped over to ours and got in the passenger side. Andy finally turned to me, "You better let me drive Zachary. You don't look too good."

I handed the keys to him and sort of shuffled off to the back seat. As soon as Andy got in the car Cynthia whistled, "This is amazing."

"Brilliant!" Andy agreed.

"What's going on?" I said, demanding attention as I leaned into the front seat.

"Are you deaf or something?" Andy asked. "Philip is taking us to his house in Bel Air."

"Why?" I spat out.

Cynthia caught the edge in my voice and answered shortly, "Because he's nice."

"He's a phoney." I mumbled.

"What?" The two of them said in unison.

"Nothing." I drawled out as I slumped into the back seat.

We followed the matching Mercedes through the heavy traffic of the city. The Hollywood hills, downtown with all its heady and exotic charm that goes right to the soul of any decent Northerner and then fabulous, opulent, awe inspiring Bel Air. I can't give you a detailed exposition of Los Angeles yet because on the initial drive through the city all I could focus on was my two companions doing a running praise session of Philip. I slumped even further in my seat, ignored.

An imposing wrought iron gate blocked the Mercedes in front of us but after a tanned forearm emerged from the tinted enclosure and pushed a few buttons on the control panel, the gates swung open and we drove up a long winding driveway. Andy and Cynthia made little oooos and aaaas as we drove up and they both let out an awed whoosh of air when they came in sight of the mansion. I said, "What's with you two? Your house is even bigger than this. You're acting like a couple of street urchins at Uncle Scrooge's house."

Cynthia gave me a dirty look but said nothing and Andy said, by way of explanation, "This is Bel Air, not Edmonton."

I let out a frustrated sigh, "What's the difference? Exchange a pine tree for a palm tree and that's it."

Neither of them answered because by then the car was parked and they practically jumped out and ran over to Philip like two dogs begging to be petted.

The three of them waited at the door for me to slowly make my way over. Andy and Philip didn't seem to notice my lack of enthusiasm as they chatted away but Cynthia scowled at me, letting me know that my time in the sun had passed. Once inside, Philip gave us the grand tour of his house, pausing at the odd conversation piece and saying things like, "I got this in Borneo." or "That was a gift from Tom Cruise." or "This was free when I bought a bowl of soup."

He led us from room to room and my two travelling companions fell deeper in love with our host with each little remark he made. Like when he mentioned this ugly looking vase that Tom Cruise had supposedly given him, Cynthia acted like she had just received twelve vitamin B shots. "Oh my God! Tom Cruise! Really?"

"Yeah," Philip sound bored as he told the story, "That was right after Jerry Mcguire. It wasn't MY film, but I did help out with the production as a favour to blah blah blah."

His diatribe lasted until we reached another room with a huge lion's head on the wall.

"You work in the movie business?" Andy's body shook with glee.

"Yeah, I've been in a few projects. Like blah blah blah."

"That has to be the coolest thing I've ever heard!"

"It's not really as exciting as it seems. Most of my time is spent blah blah blah."

He had his hands in his pockets and as he talked he swivelled around to address each of us. Every time he turned to me I looked off at something else like the thermostat, or the baseboard, or a doorknob. I was trying to convey that these household objects were a lot more interesting than him. Of course, I was being very subtle about it.

"Well sure," He said in answer to a question posed by Cynthia, "It's very rewarding. Last year when I was nominated for blah blah blah."

We ended up in the "great room". With me at the tail end of the procession, thinking bitter, mean and incredibly witty thoughts about Philip. One of the wittier things was a song with a chorus going something like, "I've had my fill of Phil, da da da, Phil makes me ill, da da da."

It was that great little song that kept me from hearing what Cynthia said to me. I snapped out of my musical trance when she poked me in the ribs with her elbow, "Zach, do you remember that movie?"
I looked up at Philip, because apparently the answer was to be addressed to him. I nodded slowly, "Yeah, that was some movie. Where's the bathroom?"
Philip pointed to a marble tiled hallway, "Third door on the left."
"Thanks Phil." I said as I sauntered off.
My not too subtle disdain was obviously noticed and I heard Cynthia apologize for me as I went down the hall. She said that I was tired or something. Yeah, tired of Philip blah blah blah.

Once in the bathroom I considered doing a number of spiteful things, like peeing on the toilet seat or rummaging around the medicine cabinet and switching around the labels on his nitro-glycerine heart medication, not that he had any medications in there anyway. I didn't do anything though. I splashed some water on my face and went back to the others, who were now seated in the "great room" listening to the "great host".

"Next week we begin filming a movie about a cult. One of the guys who ran the thing is flying down as a special creative consultant." He leaned back, assuming a snobby position on the couch. "It's a true story and aside from our artistic input, we're going to tell it like it really was."
Cynthia practically fell off the couch with glee, "Oh yeah, the cult that planted bombs all over the place! Wow! And YOU'RE making the movie about it! Who's going to be in it?"
"Brad... and Tom." He smiled dramatically, "I don't want to give anything away though."

"Brad Pitt and Tom Cruise?"

Philip looked smug but didn't say anything. I bet he kept quiet because the real actors starring in his stupid movie were Brad Jones and Tom Smith.

"Oh wow!"

I sat down next to Cynthia and she turned to me excitedly, "Did you hear that? Brad Pitt and Tom Cruise!"

"Wow." I yawned.

"But enough about me." Phillip said.

Thank God.

"What about you three? What brings you to L.A?"

Andy leaned forward, "Well Philip, we're just..." but Philip cut him off, "One sec Andrew. I want to hear all about it, but what say we go get some dinner? You must be famished after that long drive."

Andy rubbed his hands, "Sounds great. And hey, it's MY treat."

"No way Andrew, this is MY town, and I do the entertaining."

Cynthia stood up, "We can argue about it on the way, let's just get going. I'm so hungry I could eat our host."

"What did you say?" I practically screamed at Cynthia.

She looked at me like I was nuts, "I said I was hungry enough to eat a horse."

"Oh."

We all piled into one of Philip's cars. It was a silver Rolls Royce. The most pretentious automobile ever made. Lousy pretentious German automakers, I said to myself as the car pulled out of the garage.

"British." Andy whispered.

"Screw you." I thought.

Cynthia got in the front, next to Philip. My girlfriend. At least I thought she was my girlfriend. So happy to have found you, kiss you in front of the Las Vegas jailhouse girlfriend. Of course all that changed when Philip "enough about me" Donasco came driving up. So she was in the front, meaning that I was in the back. Her boyfriend. I love your brother and I love you too, kiss you in my dreams never more boyfriend. I was in the back seat. Staring holes into the back of their heads and wishing brain tumours on the both of 'em.

We went to this ultra ritzy place where even the parking attendants looked like movie stars. We got a table without delay because every waiter in the place fawned over Philip "I can get a table anytime, anywhere" Donasco. I sat between Andy and Philip "I can order for everyone because..." ah hell, you get the picture. I sat across from Cynthia and got a splendid view of her mentally undressing Philip. It made me sick and the longer I sat there not eating my unpronounceable entrée, the madder I got.

The entire conversation was nothing more than ego inflating drivel by Philip who was positively chock full of amusing name-dropping little stories. Pretty soon all talk around the table fussed into a sort of background mumble as I stewed about how I had been left out in the cold. A few hours earlier I was so down in the dumps over Andy and there he was, ignoring me.

In between the after dinner coffee and dessert I had forgotten all dreams of Cynthia and any magic that passed between us had been exposed as a fraud. She used me. What did she use me for? Who knows? A babysitter for her brother? Las Vegas companionship? A hand to be held to keep an odious lounge singer from hitting on her? Away from the glitz and into the glamour, I was a nothing sitting next to the big time Hollywood Film Maker.

If he had been in front of me in checkout lane number five, Andy would have passed me by and befriended Philip. If he had been the one standing in the casino while Andy was shooting craps, Cynthia would have taken him up to her room and did a damn sight more than ask him what his favourite nut was. The only thing he did wrong was show up eight days late. Not that it mattered, because he was there and I was the insignificant speck sitting to his left.

Why was I in that restaurant forced to listen to non-stop braggadocio and watching my only friend forget and my only love flee? Why the hell did I even go on that stupid trip? For what? For the hundred grand, oh yeah. But no, not just that, and you know it. I actually cared for that brother and sister team. Why did I care? I didn't know, because it became obvious that the puke sitting next to me in Hugo Boss evening wear had spread his infectious disease to the two starry eyed drips from Deadmonton, Alberta. They were jerks as well.

I didn't just sit there feeling left out either. I tried to reach out to my so-called friends. I would bring something up to Andy about our trip down here and he waved me off so he could listen to Philip. I smiled at Cynthia and reached for her hand across the table but she kept batting her eyelashes at Philip. Screw them, I thought. My blood boiled in spiteful and self-pitying frustration. I hated him. I hated them all. When he finally got up to go to the little producer's room Cynthia turned on me for real, "What's wrong with you Zach?"

I narrowed my eyes, "What do you mean? I'm having the time of my life."

Andy remained non-committal, spooning a huge piece of Tiramisu into his mouth.

"You're acting like a complete and utter loser." His sister spat.

I stood up, my head dizzy for some reason. "I am a complete and utter loser. Thank you for noticing."

She whispered, "Sit down, you're causing a scene."

"A scene?" I said in a way too loud tone of voice.

She hissed, "You're making a fool of yourself."

"I'm the fool?" I yelled, "No, you two are the fools! You," I pointed to Andy, "You little red haired hob goblin! You can stick your hundred grand and your friendship!"

Cynthia's jaw dropped, "And as for you! I'll get out of your way so you can pursue Philip "I've had every female lead in Hollywood" Donasco!" I threw my napkin down on the table, "It's obvious that I'm no longer needed. Andy, you got a new bodyguard, and Cynthia, you got a new boyfriend."

I turned around, stormed out of the restaurant, and melted into the dark Los Angeles night.

DAY NINE

Monday the Nineteenth

OK, I overreacted. I was jealous of Philip. I was bitter about what I perceived as Andy and Cynthia pushing me aside. I was spiteful and petty and selfish. I knew that the second I walked out of the restaurant but even knowing how terrible I was acting wasn't enough for me to repent.

That's the story of my life though. I've always been jealous, bitter, spiteful and selfish. I'm the first to admit it. When I was thirteen years old my dad took off with Wanda Whatshername and instead of dealing with it in a positive and constructive way (whatever the hell that means) I sulked and collected every tiny bit of hatred in my pubescent heart. I made up all sorts of reasons to hate my family. I hated my sisters for being such bovines, thus causing my father so much angst that he had to leave. I hated my mom for being such a cold-hearted hag, because if she had been more loving my dad wouldn't have had to seek romantic refuge with other women. Oh yeah, I hated my dad as well. The rotten prick that deserted his family for a busty secretary.

You wouldn't know that I hated them though. I kept it wrapped up inside and the only indication that I was harbouring any ill will was that I would spite them all. When my mom put her arm around my shoulders and asked me if I wanted to talk about it, I just kept on playing my video game, saying nothing. I figured that she would see how emotionally scarred I was and feel guilty about the whole thing. As much as I wanted comfort, understanding and love, I would bury those needs right next to the hate. I would sulk, pretending to be the strong one going on with life as a near catatonic victim.

I had a bit of a revelation in Psychology 271, when I first read about Freud and found out that I had a real zest for the suffering hero thing. I wanted to be the whipping boy, heaping sorrow upon myself so they could stand there and watch with guilty impotence. When I had the measles, I refused to take any medicine and even sent my mom away when she brought me chicken soup. When I went through my friendless high school years I sat conspicuously alone at lunch so I could look like some kind of tragic piece of art. Hell, the reason I've brought up all my sorrows so much is probably because I want YOU to feel sorry for me. Isn't that pathetic? You must REALLY feel sorry for me now.

Anyway, I had that Freudian Suffering Hero thing going on when I left the restaurant. I'll walk out into a dark, unknown city with no way of surviving without their help. See how that makes them feel! The jerks. That's what kept repeating itself to me as I walked toward the west. Maybe I'll end up dead on a street, the victim of some psychotic killer. A desperate junkie would slice me open with a broken bottle and sell my organs so he could get high. Boy would Andy and Cynthia feel terrible.

I walked through downtown, Beverly Hills, Santa Monica and right to the ocean. It must have been about two in the morning when I finally hit the beach and I just plopped down on the sand, feeling sorry for myself because honestly, no matter what I just said in the above paragraphs, the only person who ends up feeling sorry for the suffering hero is the hero himself.

I sat with my knees pulled up tight to my chin and stared out into the black beyond, listening to the waves and feeling cold, hungry and desperately alone. When I woke up, the sun was hidden behind a blanket of grey clouds that had rolled up from the ocean. I stood up and shook the sand out of the designer clothes that Andy had bought. I felt vindictively warm when I noticed the dirt and wrinkles on the pants and pullover.

I walked along the beach slowly and aimlessly, as I had nowhere to go and no idea how to get there. The beach was deserted except for a grey haired guy jogging with his dog. The dog, I think it was a Labrador or something, stopped to sniff at me, and the guy gave the leash a quick jerk to pull him along. At that moment I imagined Andy tugging on a leash that was wrapped around my neck, dragging me all the way from my home to California. With that less than cheerful thought in mind, I left the beach and headed down the road. I had been walking for about twenty minutes when I came to a coffee shop and after searching through my pockets and coming up with a few bucks in change, I went inside.

I bought myself a coffee with seven sandy dimes and took my steaming cup over to the corner booth and sat down. I could feel the thousand or so grains of sand that were positioned in various parts of my clothing begin to itch simultaneously so I began to scratch and fidget like a heroin addict going through withdrawal. Coupled with my dishevelled appearance, that constant scratching, rubbing and readjusting was probably what caught the eyes of the three guys who were seated directly across from me on the opposite side of the coffee shop.

Aside from the guy behind the counter, the four of us were the only people in the place and as I looked over at them I realised that they had ceased talking and were now staring at me with their three pairs of bloodshot eyes. They were all in their middle thirties and dressed in varying shades of "White Trash of Hollywood." They were wearing suits that looked like they all fell off the same truck. Wide lapel earth tone sport jackets covering even wider lapel pastel shirts. I could hear the rustle of the cheap material as they turned toward me and even though one of the guys was built like a defensive lineman, I stared back. They might have been streetwise thugs but I can be pretty surly before my morning coffee.

When they finally resumed their conversation I took out my crumbled cigarette pack and removed the last Turkish cigarette and lit it. I stared out the window as I sipped my coffee and rearranged my pants so the sand could spill out onto the floor. I drained the last bit of coffee in the cup and went back up to the counter. Holding the cup toward the guy, I asked if the refills were free. The guy shook his head, "Fifty cents for refills." I frowned and the guy said with mock sympathy, "If I didn't charge there'd be bums sitting in here all day."

I guess I did look like a bum but instead of getting into an argument all I did was slam the coffee cup down on the counter and turned on my heel like an offended consumer. I left the coffee shop with another glare at the three guys who were staring at me again. I paused once I got outside because I didn't have a clue what to do. My grand exit from the restaurant the night before had been a good show but revealed under the grey light of day I knew just how stupid I had been. What was I going to do? I had a buck thirty in change, a disposable lighter and a bad case of regret.

Before I had sufficient time to really bemoan my circumstances, I found myself surrounded by the three guys from the coffee shop. I tensed, ready to either fight or run because I figured that they were going to rob me of my precious and only belongings. The tallest and skinniest of the three was in front of me, "Hey buddy, are you alright?"

I looked from him to the other two and noticed right off that they didn't seem like the Good Samaritan type but you can never tell and I wasn't exactly the best judge of people so I let down my guard and sighed, "Not really."

The shortest of the trio cocked his head sideways in a gesture that was, I assume, meant to show sympathy but only made the guy look like a curious monkey. "What's the problem? Maybe we can help."

I didn't answer right away because I'm not totally devoid of street sense and those guys really, and I mean really, looked like something out of a Dick Tracy comic book. The skinny guy was good looking in a greasy sort of way. The kind of guy who is really forward with women and is always asking them what their sign is. He looked like a total lame - o with that cheesy suit. They all looked that way but the short one standing with one foot up on the curb looked the cheesiest with slicked back hair and a three-day beard. He was wearing three gold chains and one heavy link bracelet that hung down his wrist. The behemoth on my right just stood there looking vicious with his arms folded across his barrel chest. His clear blue eyes bore into me with a message that said that if I didn't trust him he would beat me into breakfast sausage.

The short one asked again, "What's wrong?"

I mumbled, "Nothing. I'm just going off to meet my friends. See ya."

The big guy stepped into my path, "Buddy, we're trying to help you."

I smiled, thinking that if I gave him a quick head fake I could dart to the side and run off, looking much the chicken but still retaining all my teeth and my buck thirty. "Really, I don't need help."

The greasy one cut off my escape route, "There's no reason to be afraid."

I chuckled, deciding that since running wasn't an option I might as well fake them out with a tough guy attitude. "I ain't afraid. I've just got places to go."

For some reason, whenever I try to act tough I use the word "ain't." Who uses that word nowadays? Does it sound even remotely tough outside of a James Dean movie?

"Where do ya have to go?" The short one asked.

I turned around and faced him, staring hard into his eyes, "What are you, a cop?"

Undaunted, he laughed. "Do we look like cops?"

I could feel a hundred or so grains of sand in my underwear begin to crawl around and mix with the fear that was afflicting my anatomy down there so I took a few steps forward but the big guy didn't budge.

I said, "No, you guys don't look like cops and since that means you're probably not then you can mind your own business."

(Sorry for the interruption but I guess I should tell you that the above conversation has been edited to remove most of the curse words. Those guys were really foul mouthed and if I tried to type out the dialogue verbatim, the F key on my keyboard would be worn out. In all honesty, I was using the F word a lot myself. That's another word I use a lot when the word "Ain't" doesn't cut it. I suppose it's a little more contemporary but these days, elementary school kids are using it during games of hopscotch. Basically, curses and colloquialisms are useless in trying to convey toughness and even if they did, those three guys weren't buying any of it).

The greasy guy smiled, displaying a silver incisor, "You need a fix man?"

I ignored decorum and brazenly adjusted the sand out of my crotch, "A fix?"

The big guy nodded toward the coffee shop, "It looked like you were hurting in there."

I laughed hoarsely, "I've got sand in my pants from sleeping on the beach."

The short one narrowed his eyes, "Where you from?"

"Canada," I said, immediately regretting telling those guys the truth.

"And now you're a resident of the beach." Greasy guy observed.

"Well..." I began, searching for a quick reply that would lead to an even hastier exit.

"We can help you out man." Greasy said.

"I don't need help." I said much too quickly.

"Listen," Shorty said, "You're a long way from home without any viable means of survival. L.A isn't like Canada; you'll get killed out here."

Greasy continued for him, "We can get you some cash so you can go home."

I said, "And why would you guys help me?"

The big guy smiled, "Mutual interests."

I narrowed my eyes, "What's that supposed to mean?"

Greasy gestured toward a sedan parked a few feet away. "We can talk about that on the way."

I shook my head, "Not a chance."

He laughed, "Look, if we meant to rob you we could have done that five minutes ago and you aren't cute enough to rape."

I shuddered, "Well, thanks but I don't think..."

"Five thousand bucks." Shorty spat out.

"What?"

"We'll cut you in for five thousand bucks. Enough to get home."

Five thousand bucks was enough that I wouldn't have to go home. It would be enough to buy some nice clothes, track down Andy and Cynthia and show them that I didn't need them. I would parade my independence all over the place. Then I could go home.

"What's the deal?" I asked.

"We'll talk about that on the way." The big guy said with a tight-lipped smile.

Since you're such an astute reader, you've probably figured out that those guys were up to no good and needed a patsy for some reason. You already know that they had some kind of scam planned and were looking to make me that expendable facet in their schemes. I'm not nearly as smart as you but even I knew it. You may be curious to know that I gave serious consideration to their offer. Stupid, you may be saying, but the problem I faced was that they didn't seem to want to let me go and even if I did manage to get away, what would I do? In five minutes I would be back on some curb scratching my head (and my private parts) and wondering what I was going to do.

The way I saw it, I had three choices. One, I could refuse and be back on the beach without any hope for my next meal. Two, I could refuse; head back to Philip's house in the hills and beg forgiveness from Andy. Three, I could risk possible incarceration, or even loss of life, and go with those three guys. Maybe they were on the up and up, meaning that their plan would actually make me five thousand dollars, and then I could save face with some nice duds, a good meal and a plane ticket home.

I chose the latter and indicated my choice to them by means of a shrug and a less than confident, "Ok. I'm game."

The three of them piled into the car and I got in the back seat next to Greasy. I suppose now would be the time to introduce these three upstanding members of society. The best way to do it is by height, since they seemed to be separated by the exact same amount, that being five inches. Shorty, who stood about five-five, was called Gordon. The hulk was Quentin (Five ten) and Greasy (Six three) was Leo.

The car ride began with Gordon, who was sitting in the passenger seat, lighting up a fat joint and passing it to Leo, who then in turn offered it to me. "Here, you look like you need to relax." I shook my head because the thing is, drugs would never make me relax. Paranoid schizophrenia yes, relax, no. Even at that moment I was proud that I refused the joint because the truth is, I was so scared that I probably would have accepted carrot sticks and dip if they offered, and I really hate carrot sticks.

I asked them where we were going and Gordon said that we were going back to his place to wait for a phone call. I nodded, as that seemed to make perfect sense and we drove on in silence.

We stopped in front of a decrepit tenement somewhere in the bowels of Hollywood and then we all went inside. Gordon's apartment was pretty threadbare, with one couch, one coffee table and one easy chair that bled stuffing onto the floor when I sat down in it.

I decided to cut straight to the chase, "So what is it that I'm supposed to do?"

Leo said, "You'll know when the time comes," Then he winked, "Relax, it's an easy two grand."

"Five grand." I said.

"What?" He asked.

"You said it was five grand, then just now you said…"

Gordon cut in, "It is five grand. He said five grand and you didn't hear right. And if he did say two grand, then he made a mistake, because it's five grand."

"Yeah, five grand." Leo said.

"An easy five grand." Gordon said.

Now you and I know that there's no such thing as an easy five grand, but I nodded to him and leaned back, thinking about running into Andy and Cynthia with my new clothes and new independence. "Sounds good to me." I cheerfully replied. I leaned even further back and surveyed my new friends and thought to myself that I was pretty fortunate to run into such good folk. Honestly, the more I thought about my revenge, the more I thought that maybe those guys weren't all bad. In fact, I had a brand new philosophy that had miraculously dawned on me.

What, you may ask, was my philosophy? Well, conscientious reader, it was this: I realised that I was an anti-psychic.

"What the hell does that mean?" You may also ask. (You sure do ask a lot of questions.) Simply that I discovered that I was wrong all the time so in order to be on the right path, all I had to do was go against my gut instinct. When I first met Andy, I thought that he was an irritating twit but then it turned out that he was the best friend I'd ever had. When I had embraced the fact that I loved him, he turned out to be a jerk. It was the same thing with Cynthia. She was gorgeous and I wanted her, but in reality she was a complete cow. Then I fell in love with her and thought she was a goddess but when I came to grip with that, it turned out that she really was a hag. Again, it was just like with Cherisse. What a cheap skank, I thought. But no, she was a fine and upstanding girl. What about Bobby Fabian? A complete loser, I said. Nope, wrong again! He was great guy. Philip, who you know I despised, was probably a profound artist with numerous qualities that I had missed. Therefore, I reasoned, since my first impression of Gordon, Leo and Quentin was that they were all scum; they had to turn out to be good friends. Right? But then again, if Andy really was a jerk all along and his sister was some kind of monster, then my initial judgement was right after all. Following along that line of reasoning, these three guys would be my buddies but then turn into scum, which is what I thought in the beginning. Maybe I was completely out to lunch altogether. All I do know is, that was some powerful dope they were smoking and maybe it was getting to me.

We sat around for maybe three hours, just smoking cigarettes and not talking. Even the three of them were quiet, sitting with their hands in their laps like expectant fathers in the maternity ward. After Gordon made a quick phone call they all seemed to relax and Leo went into the kitchen to make a sandwich. Meanwhile Gordon and Quentin sat on the couch facing me with snide smiles. I decided to get to know my friends a little better since the atmosphere didn't seem so tense. I said, "So, what do you guys do for a living?"

Quentin kept his smile in place, "You'll find out after we get that phone call."

"Oh."

Gordon rolled up another joint and after they filled the apartment with more smoke I managed to find out that Quentin was a bouncer who grew up in Amsterdam and could sing "Mr. Tambourine Man" in three languages. That was pretty weird, I thought. Weird, just like Andy. I was actually comforted by that fact. Gordon, when he was legit, worked in a retail paint store. He said that he could fit three dollars in quarters up his nose. Weird. Leo, who came in the room to share in the third joint, would only say that he made his living as a gigolo. "Let's just say that I don't wear extra large underwear because of my waist size." That was kind of like Andy, I thought. Y'know, the way that Andy... uh... never mind. He was nothing like Andy.

It didn't matter anyway, because I think all three of them were lying to me. Every time one of them would offer a bit of information about themselves the other two would snicker. I guess it doesn't pay to get too personal with the patsy. Besides, all similarities to my former friendship ended when a syringe was produced. Leo asked me if I wanted to join them but I shook my head no. I thought it was heroin but when I asked Gordon he just laughed and said that it was vitamins. After a round of laughter Quentin informed me that it was crystal meth and I really should have some because it would "make me sharp."

I sat there like a statue while the three of them shot up, each one offering it to me before they took their turn. I just shook my head each time and began to feel some really nasty paranoid anxiety.

Two minutes after the syringe was put away the phone rang and all three of them jumped about twelve feet in the air and Gordon made a mad dash to answer it. He nodded his head about thirty times and then hung up.

"Ok, we got ten minutes, then we gotta run."
"Is it all set?" Leo asked.
Four quick nods and then he said, "Yup. All set. It's a go."
Then he shot a look over to me and then they all converged, forming a tight little huddle about two feet away from my face.

I'm sorry to do this to you but I have to record the following in a play format otherwise my fingers would get too tired typing out who said what to whom. It all came out in rapid fire and I barely understood it all myself. Consider yourself lucky, because I had to endure it without the benefit of a written transcript.

G: Ok buddy, this is it. This is for the all the marbles.
L: Five grand, buddy. Five easy grand.
G: Yeah, listen, this is going to be simple.
Q: Real simple.
L: Like two plus two.
Q: More like one plus one.
L: What's one plus one?
Me: Two.
L: All right, it's that simple.
G: OK listen; we're going to go to a parkade downtown. There's going to be this white limo there.
L: A white caddy limo.
Q: Impossible to miss.
L: You won't miss it. It's a white limo.
G: There's gonna be this old guy there. He'll be in the back of the limo.
L: You just get in the limo.
G: In the back.
Q: With the old guy.

L: You just get right in there.

G: Yeah, right in there. He'll have something for you.

L: A package.

Q: Wrapped in paper.

L: It might be a briefcase.

Q: No, it's wrapped in paper.

G: Who cares! You just take the package.

Q: Whatever the hell it is. Briefcase or paper. You take it.

G: He's gonna ask you for a name.

Q: He's gonna ask you for a name and you tell him "Roosevelt."

L: Roosevelt. That's all you say. Roosevelt.

G: Roosevelt. Say it.

Me: Roosevelt.

Q: That's it! You just say Roosevelt and get out.

G: If he says anything else to you, you just keep your mouth shut.

Q: No, if he starts like, questioning you, you just repeat it. Roosevelt.

G: Yeah, just say it again.

L: Like you're dead serious. Look him in the eye.

G: Right in the eye.

Q: And just say Roosevelt.

G: And get the hell out.

L: If he tries to stop you...

Q: He ain't gonna try to stop him.

G: He ain't gonna do a thing.

L: But if he tries...

Q: He ain't gonna try nothin'.

G: Not a thing.

Q: Roosevelt. Say Roosevelt and get the hell out of the car.

G: Then come back to us.

L: We'll be parked around the corner.

Q: You just bring the package over to us.

L: And we'll be right around the corner.

G: We'll be right there! You just bring the stuff to us.

Q: Guess what comes next? Five grand.

L: The easiest five grand in the world.

G: A gift.

Q: Two grand, the easiest way in the world.

Me: Five grand.

Q: Yeah, five grand. What did I say?

L: Cut that out, it's five grand. That's the end of the story.

G: Got all that?

Me: Yeah.

Q: Don't say "Yeah." I mean, have you got it?

L: Repeat it.

G: Yeah, repeat it all back.

Me: Go in the parkade, look for a white limo, get in, take the package, tell him Roosevelt, get out, go around the corner...

Q: Not the parkade's corner.

L: Yeah, outside. Around the corner outside.

G: We'll be parked around the corner. Outside.

Me: Go outside, around the corner, give the package to you.

G: Collect five grand!

Me: Collect the five grand.

L: Best part of the plan right?

Q: The whole point of it all.

L: The two grand.

Me: Five grand.

G: Easiest five grand you'll ever make.

Q: A gift.

G: The whole thing takes five minutes.

L: Five minutes tops. Five minutes, five grand.

Q: If you're not back in five minutes you're dead.

L: Simple as that.

G: You're dead if you're not back in five minutes.

Q: If you even think about taking off with the package you're dead.

L: A dead man.

G: Seriously. You get back to the car in five minutes. That's it.

Q: That's all there is to it.

L: But you won't screw us.

G: Nah, you're straight up.

L: A stand up guy.

Q: A straight shooter.

G: He won't screw us around.

L: No way, he'd be dead.

Q: Dead as a doornail.

L: He won't screw us.

Q: No way.

G: Now have you got it all?

Me: Yeah.

Q: Don't say "Yeah." No messing around now. Have you got it?

Me: Yes I got it!

L: That's the answer we want.

G: That's it. Let's go.

As you can imagine, my head was spinning but I managed to follow them down to the car and get in without falling over. On the way downtown they made me repeat their instructions ten times and I was practically brainwashed by the time we got there. Gordon checked his watch and said that we were a couple minutes early and Leo replied that it was better to be too early than too late and Quentin agreed by repeating what Leo had said verbatim.

Just before it was time for me to go I asked them point blank what this was all about and Gordon snapped, "Five grand. That's what it's all about." He opened up an envelope and showed me a stack of twenties. I reached over for it but he snapped it bag closed and said with a smile, "After it's done."

"Just go in there and do it." Leo said.

"Maybe we should get him to repeat it all back." Quentin said.

"He repeated it a hundred times! He's got it! The boy isn't retarded." Gordon said.

Leo lit a cigarette, "He could be retarded and still do it perfectly."

"Repeat everything back." Quentin barked at me.

"Screw it, Q." Gordon said, "It's time for him to go."

He reached over and opened the back door for me. "Get going. If you're not back here in five minutes you're dead."

I got out of the car and walked across the street into the parkade and looked around. There it was, the white limo parked way in the back all by it itself. I took a deep breath and started toward it. My mind was going a million miles an hour trying to figure what it was all about. Who was the old man in the car? What was in the package? Why was he giving it to me? Why weren't one of those guys doing this? Why why why?

I was about halfway to the limo when all of a sudden a black car stopped in between the limo and me. I panicked for a second because I thought it was the cops but cops don't drive around in a black Mercedes.

The window glided down, "Zachary! What the hell?"

You guessed right. It was Andy.

I sneered, "Ain't you dead yet?" (Sorry, those guys were a bad influence on me. Last appearance of the word "Ain't". I promise). I walked around his car and made a quick beeline for the limo.

I opened the back door and got in without looking back to see if Andy was still there. I sat down next to an old bald guy wearing an expensive suit. He was holding a plastic grocery bag on his lap. Sitting opposite us was a younger man, maybe in his forties, wearing dark sunglasses. The old man glared at me, "Where is he?"

"Roosevelt."

"What's that supposed to mean?"

"Roosevelt," I said quickly.

"I don't know what that means."

"Roosevelt," I said again. "Give me the package."

"Not until you answer me!" He was really getting steamed.

"Roosevelt." I started to feel more embarrassed than scared.

"What the hell is that supposed to mean?" He asked the man across from us.

"The Roosevelt Motel?" The dark sunglasses guy asked me.

"Give me the package." I repeated.

The old man sort of flung it into my lap and I could feel that there were stacks of money in the bag. I opened the door but the old man had his hand on my arm, "If you double cross me I'll kill you." I pulled free and got out of the car. Andy was still parked in the middle of the lane but I walked right past and out the building.

The three guys in the car started the engine when they saw me approach and Gordon held a white envelope in his hand. He rolled down the window, "Give me the bag."

I handed it to him through the open window and he gave me the envelope. "Easiest money you'll ever make." He said and then the car roared off down the street.

I stood there like a dope before I thought to look in the envelope. Inside was a solitary Twenty Dollar bill. Damn.

Nevertheless, I crammed the envelope into my pocket and the black Mercedes pulled up beside me. The passenger window rolled down. "What was that all about?"

I shrugged.

"C'mon Zachary, get in."

I opened the door with a sigh and I felt like an utter zero as I plopped down into the familiar leather seat.

He started off and he asked me again, "Where have you been?"

I shrugged again.

"Why did you freak out last night?"

Once again, I shrugged.

"What just happened back there?"

The shrug.

"I really missed you Zachary. We were pretty worried about you."

I didn't acknowledge him. I turned toward the window and just stared out.

We drove on in silence for a few blocks and then I said, "Where are we going?"

"Home." He said.

DAY TEN

Tuesday the Twentieth

I'd like to tell you what was going through my mind when I first got in the car with Andy but for the life of me, I don't remember. I know I was glad to see him but we didn't exchange mushy pleasantries or heartfelt hugs. I was still embarrassed so I looked out the window and watched the houses, and the buildings, and more houses and finally black highway.

Wait, I know one thing that I was thinking about. Cynthia. I pictured her in Philip's arms. Her beautiful eyes staring into his as he told her how he was going to put her in the movies and that she would be a big star. Sometimes I have a pretty good imagination and every bit of it was used in creating gruesome images like her and Philip sipping wine out of crystal goblets that reflected the candle light in Phillip's bedroom. I shut my eyes but the pictures became clearer. "Oh Cynthia..." Philip's manly voice would croon, "Would you like to see my bathtub? It fits two." Sometimes my imagination can be pretty cheesy.

We passed Oxnard, Ventura and Santa Barbara. As a few more miles peeled away I turned my mind back to the present and wondered if Andy and I were driving home without Cynthia. Good Lord above! Maybe my imagination wasn't being too imaginative! Maybe Cynthia really was staying in Hollywood to star in movies and share a bathtub!
"Andy! Where the hell are we going?"
He didn't answer and despite what my mind was churning out, I didn't ask again.

The sun was casting a long orange and red blanket over the ocean and before it melted away, Andy turned off the road and shut the car off.

"What are we doing Andy?" I asked a little more forcefully as the engine clicked a lonely rhythm as it gave off heat.

"Come see the ocean with me." He said as he opened the door.

I followed him down a short, manageable grade to the rocky beach below. We walked to a small promontory and he climbed onto a large boulder that withstood the rush and crash of the waves that sprayed water almost to the peak of the rock.

With some huffing and puffing I followed him up and sat down next to him. He took out a cigarette and offered me one. I took it and let him light it for me. After letting the smoke curl upwards from his lips he let out a long sigh.

"They say life began in the oceans. I don't know if that's true but if you really look at it, you can almost feel the power of life coming from it."

The sound of the waves and the smell of the air seemed to pacify me and the first calm thought I had was of how rotten I had behaved. I looked out at the broad expanse and I wanted to apologize to him for everything. I was just about to do just that but he quietly looked out at the ocean and said, "I'm glad you're here with me to see this." I was going to reciprocate right after a quick confession of my sins but he spoke again, "Forget about yesterday. Let's just be friends again." He stuck out his little white hand and I shook it, surprised at how cold he was.

"Hey man, do you want me to go back to the car for a jacket or something?"

He shook his head, "Nah, let's just sit for a while."

We sat for a long time, listening to the waves and smoking cigarettes. The sunset gave way to moonlight that sent a long white beam reflecting on the water. When we did speak we didn't talk about my behaviour, or Philip or even Cynthia. We talked about movies, books, music and other mundane things that friends talk about in settings somewhat less magnificent.

Except, around two in morning, after Andy told me some lame joke about blondes and screwing in a light bulb, I pulled a non sequitur and said, "Hey man, I've really been wondering about something."

"What's that?" He asked with a bit of a smile as he was still chuckling over his joke.

"What's with you and those showers?"

He sighed, "It's kind of quirky isn't it?"

"Dude, everything about you is quirky. But the shower thing sticks out."

"Well, did you ever read Macbeth?"

"Are you telling me that you have something like a Lady Macbeth syndrome?"

"Sort of. She was always washing her hands to get the blood off and I..."

Because his voice trailed off I said, "You don't have to tell me if you don't want to."

He looked up the sky. "Let's just say that I feel guilty over my parents. We didn't part on good terms."

Like I said earlier, I'm not any good at being consoling or sympathetic. I said, in a tone of voice that sounded way too glib, "So you have all these showers as a form of penance?"

He smiled. "No, I shower because I appreciate good personal hygiene."

I softened my tone, "I'm sorry about your folks."

"Me too." He turned to me and all of a sudden, he didn't look ugly at all. "You're not lonely any more are you?"

I shook my head, feeling tears come to my eyes. "Thank you Andy."

"For what?"

"For stopping me in the grocery store, for making me spend the night at your house, for making me come to California. Thank you for being my friend."

He gripped my shoulder and gave it a fatherly squeeze. "Don't thank me, Zachary. I was just about to thank you for the same thing."

I took a quick breath. "Don't die Andy."

He let out a soft laugh. "We all have to die sometime."

"Sometime is fine. Just not here, not now, not... not until we get back home." That sounded incredibly stupid and I wanted to say more but Andy cut me off, "It's not exactly my decision to make you know."

"Yeah, but you can see the future, right? You're a prophet or a psychic or whatever so you have to know when you're going to die! You do know don't you?"

He smiled again. "Of course I know when I'm going to die. I'll die when it's my time to die."

"Ah man," I said, full of disgust, "You know damn well what I mean. I've felt this dread over you dying since Vegas, just thinking about L.A being your last hurrah and I just can't bear the thought of you being gone!"

He sat there for a few minutes without saying anything and just before I was about to speak he said, "I've woken up every day wondering if that day was going to be my last one, but for all I know I could live another hundred years. You should think that way too. And Zachary, one more thing."

"Yeah?"

"Stop being so depressing! You're starting to annoy me! No more talk about me dying, OK? You promise me now."

I shook my head.

"Promise me." His voice was firm. "Every day we're all faced with death. You, me and everybody. So don't sit there focusing on mine as if it's such a big deal and before you argue with me and say that it is, I'm just saying that I don't want to hear about it. OK? So stop it."

"OK." I said sadly.

"Promise me not to bring it up again."

"I promise."

"Good, now did you hear the one about…"

He told me another joke about a priest, a rabbi and a Buddhist monk. We laughed, we talked some more and we sat silently; all blended together in seamless moments. All night, without feeling too cold, or too tired, or wanting to be anywhere else in the world.

When the sun began to creep up behind us, Andy stood up and stretched, smiling his gap tooth, hideous smile. I smiled back. "Hey, how about some breakfast? My treat. All you can eat for twenty bucks."

He shook his head, "Sorry, I've got a big day ahead. You can have breakfast with Cynthia."

I stuck my hands in my pockets, "Do you really think she'll even stay in the same room as me after how I left the other night?"

He turned to me with those pale blue eyes and looked at me like I was the stupidest man alive. "Zachary, she loves you. Haven't you got that through your thick head yet?"

My only answer was to bow my head. I felt embarrassed and ashamed. I'd done nothing to earn her love and the pain of what I expected was easier to take than the shame of getting what I hadn't dared to hope for.

"If you love her too, you have to stop being such a moron."

"It's all I know how to be." I said with a small smile.

"Maybe it's time you learned something else." He said with a straight face.

I coughed in my fist, "Well, I've learned not to sit on a rock all night without a jacket."

"See? Another lesson learned."

"And when are you going to start teaching me something important? When do we start on the big things?"

He smiled, "I've been teaching you those things all along."

I gave him a wry smile, "Well, you haven't done a very good job. I still don't know anything."

He smiled again. "I'm not so sure about that."

Before I could disagree he cast one final look at the ocean below us and hopped down off the rock toward the road. I followed him to the car and I paused before getting in, "So, no breakfast?"

He shook his head, "Nope. Busy day."

I smiled, "Like what? Disneyland? Universal Studios? Mann's Chinese Theatre?"

He laughed, "Nah, no touristy stuff for me."

"So what then? A drink at the Whiskey A Go Go? I'd be up for that."

He shook his head again, "No. Take Cynthia out. Have some fun."

I got in the car with a sigh and when he started the engine I said, "Do you really think everything will be OK with Cynthia and I?"

He didn't seem to hear as he turned the car around and headed back south along the highway.

"Andy?"

"What?"

"I asked you if you think everything will work out with Cynthia."

He let out an exasperated breath. "You acted like an idiot, but sometimes that's all part of love. You have to purge out the garbage before you get to the gold."

I laughed, "Did you get that off a fortune cookie?"

He smiled, "Nope, that's an Andy Tiernan original."

"Are you sure you don't want to go Mann's? We could get you a job there."

We drove back to LA without talking about anything important. It was just me saying things like, "Hey, look at that girl!" and "Whoa, check out that car!" Just a sightseer and a seer in a strange city. Andy stopped in front of a hotel that had a nice view of the Hollywood sign and said, "Here's where you get off."

I looked up at the hotel, "What's this?"

"Cynthia's in room 316."

"You're not coming up?"

He shook his head, "No. You two should be alone."

I stared down at the ground. "I'm scared Andy."

Now, you may be wondering why I was scared. Well, so was I. I don't know why I felt afraid and I don't know why I told Andy. I knew he would only have some wise one liner to say but that's just one more example of fate. Sometimes you say stuff without knowing why only to find out that it opened some doorway to destiny. Or maybe your heart is the one doing the talking and for once your mouth finally obeyed. Anyway, Life is weird that way.

Andy looked me with a solemn gaze and said, "You don't have to be."

I nodded, "I know but..."

"But you are, and that means that whatever happens from now on is real and important. Otherwise you wouldn't be scared. But in this, you don't have to have any fear. Trust me."

I only nodded in reply and got out of the car. I paused and leaned back inside, "You never told me what you're doing today."

He said, "I'm going to make it rain."

I looked up toward the bright blue sky and smiled, "I don't think you're going to have much luck."

"We'll see." He said.

Before I closed the door I said, "I won't even bother to figure that one out. See ya later, and dinner is on me tonight. Don't forget."

I walked around the car toward the entrance and I could hear Andy's window slide down. "Zachary."

I turned around to face him and my heart almost burst at the sight of tears on his cheeks. He said, "I get scared too."

There were a hundred things that my heart wanted to say. No, a thousand, maybe a million. But my tongue was a coward and all I did was stand there dumb as he drove away without looking back.

What did he mean about making it rain? Why was Andy, the ever joyful and brave, scared? I couldn't even think, because the Mercedes disappeared around a corner and the front entrance loomed up large before me. Cynthia was inside, and at least I knew why I was afraid.

I went through the lobby to the stairs and slowly climbed the three flights. The hallway of the third floor was carpeted with this ultra thick red carpet that absorbed each footfall and made the journey toward 316 seem like a dream. You can't imagine all the thoughts that were racing through my head as I walked down that hallway. Every word I had heard Cynthia speak and every physical feature in hard edged detail. I thought about each time we were together and of course, the last time I had seen her. I thought about Philip and his perfect everything and I knew that I couldn't compete. Andy, the supposedly infallible prophet was wrong; she couldn't love me. Not with a world full of guys just as great as Philip that she could have with a smile.

It would be wrong for me to love her. I didn't deserve her. It was as simple as that.

But I loved her. I really did. I was ready to give her up and isn't that the greatest form of love? To give away what's most dear? But... what if we were meant for each other? What if she really did love me? A thousand buts later I looked up at the doors that I passed and tried not to think. 308,310,312,314... I took a deep breath and stared at the black letters on the door. I closed my eyes and said my first prayer since elementary school. Then I knocked.

My heart ticked off the milliseconds and a thousand beats thumped in my chest. Words are so slow, but thoughts can move at the speed of light. A million more scenarios passed through my mind at lightning speed. When the door swung open she looked so beautiful I couldn't breathe. In one day I had almost forgotten just how gorgeous she was. When she saw me her eyes opened a little wider and before I had time to fall to my knees and beg her forgiveness I found myself in her arms.

She held me tight and it was Heaven. It was a feeling so great and wonderful that I didn't know whether to cry or laugh. It turned out to be closer to the former because all of a sudden she let go, took a step back and punched me in the stomach. It wasn't a girlie type of punch either. She really hauled off and nailed me. I gripped my stomach and swallowed back the urge to vomit. Tears came to my eyes and I blinked through them as I looked up at her.

"You've got some nerve!" She practically yelled at me.
Through clenched teeth I moaned, "I'm sorry."
She grabbed my shoulder and pulled me into the apartment. I let go of my gut and tried to pretend that it didn't hurt but holy, I really needed to sit down.

With a grimace that I was sure was all too noticeable, I stood up straight and looked at the love of my life stand with her hands on her hips and a scowl that seemed to drive the temperature of the room down.

"So where were you?"

I shrugged, trying to buy some time before I had to speak. You see, after getting punched in the gut your voice betrays just how much pain you're undergoing.

"Are you going to answer me?"

I rubbed my sore belly, "Just as soon as I catch my breath."

"You've been gone two days! You insult everybody and then you just take off for two days!"

She turned and went over to the TV that happened to be tuned to a daytime talk show, presumably dealing with the topic of "Jerks, and the women who punch them in the gut." She flicked the TV off and then turned back to me, "You really had me fooled Zach. I thought you were different. I thought you cared about me."

"I do care about you!" I sputtered.

She shook her head, "No you don't. If you cared you wouldn't have said the things you said. You wouldn't have just taken off like that for any reason!"

As much as I wanted to be supplicating and contrite, my need to be justified was starting to get an edge on my repentance.

"No reason? You were draped all over Philip Whatshisname! You didn't even know I existed once he cruised up!"

She had a look of incredulity, "Are you insane? He helped us out of that jam and I was merely being nice to him."

"HA!" I spat out. "You were on him like a second skin!" I fluttered my eyelashes in mockery, "Oh Philip, DO tell us about your fabulous movie! Oh Philip, PLEASE let us repay you." I scowled, "It was pathetic."

I expected her to launch herself across the room to deck me after my verbal stabbing but she smiled instead. "You're jealous."

My mouth dropped in indignation, "I'm not jealous!"

She smirked, "You are SO jealous."

"Yeah well, you can think whatever you like." I said.

Her smile disappeared, "So why did you take off then? If you weren't jealous why did you run away?"

"I didn't run away!"

"No? What would you call it then?"

I looked down at my shoes, then at the ceiling, then over to the potted palm in the corner of the room. Then I sighed, "Ok, I ran away. I was jealous and I ran away. I just needed to be alone so I could think."

Her voice was a little bit softer, "And did you think?"

"Yeah, I did."

I didn't say any more and her voice rose once again, "And what did you think about?"

I shrugged, "Stuff."

"Stuff! You were gone for two days! I was worried sick! I mean I was physically ill with worry! I threw up five times yesterday because I thought something horrible had happened to you!"

It was my turn to smile, "You were worried about me."

A look of shocked realisation came to her face, "I wasn't REALLY worried."

"You just said you were worried sick!"

She looked down at her feet, the ceiling and the little table near the phone. "Ok, I was worried." Her eyes snapped over to me, "Because I care about you! I sat here while you were out THINKING! I hope those thoughts were worth it!"

I started walking toward her and her features softened with each step. "They were. I thought about how much I love you." I took her hands and kissed them, "I was just so afraid."

There were precious tears in her eyes, "Afraid? Of losing me?"

I shook my head, feeling tears coming to my own eyes, "No. Of keeping you." I pressed her hands against my chest, "I was angry when I saw you with Philip but I realised that he, or someone like him, would be a lot better for you. God Cynthia, you deserve the greatest guy in the world. Not someone like me."

I let go of her hands but she held on, "I love you too Zach. I don't want Philip or the million other guys like him. I want you."

I didn't even look at her, "How can you? Look at me for God sakes."

She turned my head towards her, forcing my eyes to look into hers, "I am. Do you know what I see? I see a man who cares, who feels. I see a guy that would step up and get his butt kicked in order to help a friend. I see a guy that can be funny and loving and brave, all at the same time. I'm not a seer like Andy, who saw those things in you right away, but it didn't take me long to realize how amazing you are. Zach, you're beautiful." She kissed me so softly that I saw spots. Like the very first time I had ever tasted a kiwi fruit. Like the first touchdown pass I caught. It was even like the night Andy and I stayed up in my hotel room till four am, talking and joking around and feeling... loved. Also for the first time.

We held each other tight and then after what seemed like a blissfully long time, she laughed and said, "How come whenever we have these great reunions you smell so bad?"

I laughed despite my protest, "Hey, you'd smell too if you spent the last two nights sitting by the ocean!"

Her eyes registered concern, "Oh, you poor thing." She kissed me again and then said, "I want to hear all about it but first..."

I smiled, "I know, I know, right after I have a shower. You're starting to sound like your brother."

Her eyes opened wide once again, "Oh my God, I forgot about Andy! He was out looking for you! I haven't seen him since yesterday!"

She was starting to freak out so I quickly took her hand, "It's OK. He found me yesterday. He was the one who dropped me off. How else did you think I would know where to find you?"

She laughed, "I thought maybe you were becoming psychic."

I shook my head, "No way, too much responsibility."

After a few more mild jokes, sexy looks and a couple bashful smiles, I went to have a shower. Since the woman that I was in love with also happened to love me, we showered together. Before you get the wrong idea, I'm not mentioning the fact that we showered together because of some infantile need to share my sexual exploits. If I really were so ungentlemanly, I would forego my rules about descriptive novels and write about every soap covered lurid detail. No, the real reason is because while we were together, I had a moment. A MOMENT.

On the first day of kindergarten, when my mom waved good-bye and the teacher sat me down in front of a finger painting set, I had A MOMENT. I was no longer a baby. The apron strings were cut and I was out there in the real world and what's more, I knew it. I mean I really KNEW it.

The same thing happened when I went to a school dance and got ripping drunk behind the gym with some guys from the twelfth grade. I wasn't a kid anymore. I was out there in the real world once again. Another MOMENT. You can call them moments of self-actualisation or supra conscious landmarks or gestalts. Whatever. I had one in the shower with Cynthia.

I didn't know what I was or what I had become, but I knew that the world was different. I was different. I was beyond happy. I was in that state of bliss that is tinged, only slightly tinged mind you, with sadness. Sadness that floats on the outside of reality so that it has lost its bite and is only a warm kind of ache that reminds you of the horrors of yesterday and then affirms that they are gone forever. Not only the bad things vanish, but the shell of the good as well. Something special, something necessary, some building block was lost and gone for good. Putting away childhood things, shedding a skin, knowing that the bread crumbs that I'd left on the path to find my way back were eaten by birds but then knowing, in a beautiful flash of emotional light, that it didn't matter because I was already home.

Confused? I'm sorry, but that's the only way I can describe it. The weirdest thing of all was that Cynthia felt it too. I could tell right away. Her eyes opened wider, a smile spontaneously appeared, and goose bumps rose under hot water. We didn't talk about it till much later, but we both just KNEW. Something was gone, but what had appeared not only filled the gap, but also gave honour to what had passed away. Still confused? Ok, one final analogy in a last ditch effort to let you into my heart: Do you remember your favourite childhood toy? Think of the one that you played with more than all the others. It was probably the greatest symbol of youthful innocence and the one where you would cry if it were to be taken away. Can you picture it? Now I'll ask you another question: How often do you play with it now? You see, the childhood gems are only great memories. The toys are broken, lost or put away in some attic and we don't cry anymore when they aren't around. We smile when we think of them but we don't need them anymore. I wasn't sure what precious gem I lost when I was in the shower but I knew that it was time to put it away. The great and noble desire had been quenched.

So, with our eyes shining, hearts beating and hair smelling of herbal shampoo, Cynthia and I left her room and took a leisurely tour of L.A. We cruised around the city without a care in the world. We talked, we laughed, and we held hands and kissed as we sat on a bench near a playground. We were oblivious to the kids who cracked jokes and pointed their fingers at us. Hell, we were oblivious to the whole world.

I told her about my adventure with the three crooks and how Andy and I had spent the night looking out at the ocean. She told me how Philip had offered her a small role in one of his movies but that she refused. She told me that as the evening wore on, she began to see what an egotistical jerk he was and neither she nor I could understand why Andy had latched onto him.

The day kept floating by as we took the bus downtown. On Hollywood Boulevard we watched a guy draw a caricature of William Burroughs smoking a joint and a street preacher proclaim to all willing ears that Jesus was black. We had supper at a cosy Italian restaurant and forgot about everything that walked or crawled on the planet. Cynthia paid the bill and I suddenly remembered that I had promised Andy dinner. "I hope he isn't mad." I said over a bowl of soft chocolate ice cream.
"We'll bring him a doggie bag." Cynthia said.
"Maybe we can take him out to a movie or something."

"That's a good idea."

We took a cab back to the hotel and once we were in the lobby Cynthia had a mild revelation that made her stop walking. "Do you know what I just realised? Andy never got a room for himself. He dropped me off and said that he was going to look for you. He told me to get a room but..."

"And you didn't think to get one for him?"

She shook her head, "No. The thought never occurred to me." She looked at me with her eyes open a little wider, "Isn't that odd?"

"Yeah, kind of spooky actually."

She touched my arm, "Do you really think so? Because that's the kind of feeling that I'm getting right now."

I didn't have an answer for her but it didn't matter because she didn't wait for one. She quickly went over to the reception desk and asked the clerk if Andy had checked in. When the snotty little punk told her that he couldn't give out that kind of information she gave him a cold stare and asked him if he wanted to know what his spleen looked like when separated from his body. He smiled nervously as his thin fingers typed away at the computer in front of him. After squinting at the screen a few moments he said, "I'm sorry miss, there's no one registered under that name."

Cynthia then asked if there were any messages for her and again he shook his head. She turned to me with a worried look and said, "Let's go wait in my room. He's bound to call right away."

We ordered a pot of tea from room service and sat around trying to not look worried. We looked at the clock, ticking off dreadful minutes with a glowing red display that seemed to be laughing at us. We tried in vain to find something to talk about that would take our minds off the growing anxiety but when the sun went down, we didn't even try to mask our worry.

"Where did Andy say he was going?" Cynthia asked me for the tenth time.

"He said that he was going to make it rain."

"What does that mean?"

"I don't know."

"Where do you think he is?"

"I don't know."

She got to her feet, "Damn it! Where the hell is he?"

It went on like that for the next three hours. Sometimes she asked the same questions, sometimes I did, but neither of us had the answers. We paced the floor; we drank four pots of tea and smoked two packs of cigarettes.

At ten o'clock Cynthia stood up resolutely and said, "Well, Andy will kill me for this but I'm phoning the police."

I nodded, "That's a good idea."

She dialled the number and told the operator that she wanted to report a missing person and while she was on hold she and I exchanged lines like, "I'm sure it's nothing but just to make sure." and "He probably had some car trouble." or "He might have met someone with the Vibe."

When someone came on the line Cynthia gave them a description of Andy and of the Mercedes. She told them every little detail including the brand of cigarettes that Andy was smoking. I'm sure the cop had stopped paying attention long before but Cynthia sounded so distraught that he must have been humouring her.

After hanging up the phone Cynthia sighed, "He said that they can't do anything until he's been missing twenty four hours."

I went over to her and kissed her cheek, "Everything will be OK." What a lame thing to say but it's all anybody can ever come up with in those situations.

She was crying so I took her by the hand and led her over to the couch. We sat there sniffling and thinking the darkest thoughts that had ever crossed our minds. Almost an hour passed before I had a bit of a revelation, "We could try the hospitals."

Cynthia just wiped a tear away and nodded. I went over to the phone but before I could pick it up it rang.

I scooped it up before the ring finished, "Andy?"

"This is Sergeant Pilotte of the California Highway Patrol. May I speak with Cynthia Tiernan?"

I held the phone out to Cynthia who was already standing beside me. She took the phone in her trembling hand and pressed it to her ear. She nodded once, and then spoke a feeble affirmative. She stared down at the floor and then nodded again. Her eyes were shut and her knuckles grew white against the receiver. The trembling began in her hand, worked its way up her arm and quickly overtook her entire body.

She said good-bye and attempted to hang up the phone. I came over and took it from her and replaced it in the cradle. The tears were pouring and her mouth tried to form words that never made it out.

I held her and stroked her hair but I had to know. I had to know if I had to cry as well. "Cynthia, what is it? Is Andy ok?"

She shook her head, "He wouldn't tell me much, just that there was an accident. The police are waiting downstairs."

I tried to be casual, "Hey, maybe he wasn't hurt. Maybe he just got arrested again."

She shook her head and more tears came, "No. It's something worse, I know it is."

She started to cry in earnest and I had to practically carry her to the elevator. She kept her head on my shoulder the whole way down and when the elevator stopped she stood up, straightened her clothes and lifted her chin. She looked so brave and beautiful that my heart squeezed against my ribs. It was that heartbreaking.

Two cops were waiting at the desk, one muscular guy with a neatly trimmed moustache and his butchy looking female partner. They both wore nicely practiced looks of sympathy but they said nothing. The lady cop took Cynthia by the arm and led her outside.

I followed with the other cop a few paces behind and whispered to him, "What happened?"

He wouldn't say anything. He just kept walking with his eyes straight ahead like he hadn't heard me.

We got to the police car and Cynthia held my hand again as we got in the back. No one spoke as we drove away even though I wanted to drill questions until I struck some answers. I expected Cynthia would do the same but she slumped against me, defeated. It was as if she already knew every black detail.

We pulled up to the hospital entrance and went inside. When we reached the desk the female cop took Cynthia by the arm again and led her down a hallway away from me. I would have been right beside them but the other cop put his hand on my shoulder and said, "You can't go. Just wait here."

I looked at the cop's nameplate and said, "Sergeant Pilotte, please tell me what's going on."

He shook his head, "I can't say just yet." He gave my shoulder a friendly squeeze and then left me standing there.

I stared down the hallway long after Cynthia had gone and then I went over to a waiting area and sat down. Twenty minutes later two more cops came in and they went over to talk to Sergeant Pilotte. They smiled as they talked and I could make out some parts of their conversation. They were making jokes about some drug dealer who tried to out run the cops on a skateboard and how they had to shoot him in the knee to catch him. After that jocular tale ended they asked Pilotte why he was there. I didn't catch what he said at first but I stood up and casually made my way over to them so I could hear. Pilotte was leaning against a post holding a Styrofoam cup of coffee and smiling, "It was crazy. Right out in the middle of the Mojave, nothing there but this black Mercedes flipped over, smashed to hell and sitting upside down. The kid was dead as a doornail. " I could feel my stomach start to heave.

"But it was the damnedest thing." Sergeant Pilotte added, "Right out there in the Mojave Desert... it was raining."

DAY ELEVEN

Wednesday The Twenty-first

Andy was dead.

Cynthia identified the body and when she came out of the morgue, she was leaning heavily on the policewoman. She found me slumped in a chair, staring at her with what must have been vacant eyes.

I stood up when she came close and we both collapsed into each other. I remember her arms holding me tightly and her face pressed against my chest. She was crying so much that I could feel my T-shirt dampen.

What I don't remember is anyone else in the world existing. How we got back to the hotel is a mystery. All I can clearly recall are Cynthia's tears, my tears and how cold the room was. We held each other. We kissed each other's salty lips and moaned in pain and loss. We crawled into bed and held on tight. We didn't speak that whole day. We just held on. And we cried.

DAY TWELVE

Thursday The Twenty Second

When I woke up I heard the shower going. The sun was shining and the hotel's air conditioner was already humming, sending cold air rippling across my chest. I sat up, feeling like I had just finished a weeklong bender. Everything was blurry and disjointed, like the kind of dreams you get when you have a fever of a hundred and two.

I sat up and swung my legs out of bed, sending blood rushing to my cobwebbed brain. I rubbed my eyes and leaned over to reach the pack of cigarettes that sat on the table next to the bed. I lit one and inhaled deeply, feeling the head rush reach a crescendo before I let the smoke drool out of my mouth.

After I finished the cigarette I still didn't move. I kept my head bowed and my hands on my knees as I tried to grasp a thin strand of reality. Andy's death was surreal, a two day scene from a Cronenberg movie. Even the sound of the shower shutting off and the incessant hum of the air conditioner seemed like far off reminders of normalcy.

Do you remember the dream I had way back in Chapter two? I must have had that same dream about twenty times the previous night and it left me sweating despite the cold of mourning. I saw the highway illuminated by two halogen headlights. I heard the engine roar and the floorboards shake beneath my feet. The speedometer reached one fifty, a cactus on the left tore asunder and I saw Andy's reflection in the rear-view mirror where my face should have been. Rain poured down and the pavement rose up in defiance of gravity. Once, twice, three times and then the car flipped too fast for me to count how many more times the asphalt crashed into the night sky.

Even in the sunlight that squeezed through tightly drawn curtains, my mind went back to the dark night that took my only friend. I stared hard at the white wall across the room to blank out the thoughts but it served as a projection screen, displaying the spectral image in recurring clarity.

In case my pathetic prose is too subtle, what I mean to say is that I was going nuts. It wasn't enough that a piece of my soul was missing, but my mind was also taking a leave of absence. I sincerely hope that you yourself will never have to go through anything like that. Even if you're the biggest jerk to walk the planet, I wouldn't wish that kind of madness on you. No one deserves that kind of thing.

Suddenly, and without warning Cynthia came into the room all dressed and her still wet hair tied back. I looked up at her helplessly and knowing instantly that she saw that I was still out of it. She came over to me with her lips pressed tightly together. She hugged me, pressing my face against her bosom and I could feel her steady heartbeat. Long before I was ready to let go she released me and gave me a gentle kiss on the forehead. Then she knelt down in front of me and said, "It's a new day."

I think it was the first coherent words that she had spoken in the last 36 hours. I was amazed at the strength in her voice and the rock solid steadiness of her piercing eyes. I felt so weak in comparison and conflicting thoughts came to me in a rush. I was envious of Cynthia's strength and yet I was judgemental at the same time, feeling that she should still be a basket case. A day wasn't enough to mourn. The way I felt, a lifetime wasn't enough.

"I went through your mail."
I blinked twice, "What?"

She stood up and went over to the chair that my suitcase rested against; it was open, the top flopped against the chair. She bent down and picked up a thin sheaf of papers that were tied together with string. She brought it over to me and placed it on my lap delicately. I looked down and knew immediately that it was from Andy, written on various types of motel stationary. Cynthia said, "I wasn't going to tell you that I read it. I tied it in the string the way I found it. I wasn't even going to read it in the first place but I was too curious. He left it for you and I figured that it would hold some kind of clue."

"Does it?"

She nodded, "I think so."

She stooped down and kissed me quickly on the lips and then turned around, picking up her light blue jacket from the closet and going to the door. She swung the jacket on, flicking her hair out of the way and looked at me solemnly, "I'm going out for a walk. I think it would be for the best if you read them without me here."

I felt my voice croak, "Are you coming back?" For some reason, I felt like everything that mattered was sifting away from me and I honestly felt that I would never see her again.

She looked shocked, "Of course I'm coming back." She paused like she was going to say something else and then with her hand lingering on the doorknob she said, "I love you Zach."

Her words were a salve, a magic potion from Heaven. I sat up straighter, "I love you too Cynth."

After a quick smile she opened the door and was gone.

I stared at the door and listened for any footsteps but there was nothing but the hum of the air conditioner and the beat of my heart. I looked down at the tidy bundle of papers that sat on my lap.

"Dear Zachary"

I felt better that fast. Just seeing the strokes of his pen and imagining his squeaky voice saying my name made me feel like everything that had happened over the past two days was a dream.

He was alive again, just like that. I don't mean that he was like this ghost or anything. He was alive, somewhere, just not here, where you and I live.

"By the time you read this I'll be dead. I always wanted to say that!!! I hope that the period of morbid mourning is over and you feel better. You have Cynthia now and you two will have a great... wait, I'm not saying anything more on that. It's hard being able to see things and know what's going to happen. But I won't even say more about that either! Not just yet anyway.

I don't really know what to write though. Isn't that odd? Two minutes ago I practically tripped over the bed in my hurry to get over here and write. I had a million things to say and now that I'm here holding the pen my mind is blank. There are a million things I want to tell you but I know there are maybe only ten things that I SHOULD tell you.

First of all, I want to say thanks. Thanks for coming on this trip. I know that it must have taken a leap of faith for you to just drop everything and come along. It wasn't the money was it Zachary? I mean, you wouldn't have agreed to come if not for the hundred grand but now that you're here... now that you've been behind the wheel and felt the wind in your hair and now that we've talked and spent time together and become friends... anyway, if it was the money I hope that it isn't now. Seriously, because I never wrote you a cheque.

"Little creep." I said out loud, but I was smiling as I said it.

I have this great riff going through my head. It happens to me every night. I'll lie down and then this song will come to mind and I'll be pacing the floor humming it and thinking about... everything. I don't sleep much anymore. I find that I don't need sleep at all. There's too much to think about and I dream when I'm awake. But more on that later!!!

Did I ever tell you that I had a rotten childhood? There was a bully in every grade from kindergarten until grade twelve and whoever that bully was, he picked on me. What made it worse was that I could hear their mean thoughts before they spoke them. I could hear every girl cringe and every guy laugh. I was an easy target as you can well imagine and the only person who ate lunch or played with me at recess was Cynthia. With her looks she could have been the most popular girl in the world but she turned her back on the whole world to be my friend. Until you came along, she was the only friend I had ever had.

Are you feeling sorry for me yet? Well stop right now. I used to feed off sympathy. I used to be the ultimate suffering hero and when I think back on that, I just want to puke. I've only been really alive since I found out I was going to die.

I realised that my whole life has just been a blink. If I lived for a hundred more years it would still be a blink. I used to love reading the comics because Snoopy would always be best friends with Woodstock and Lucy would never catch a fly ball. I loved that they never changed and never would. It was a rock, a constant, something that you could always count on. But life isn't like that and if you think about it, it's a good thing that it isn't. I for one would like to see Charlie Brown grow up and marry the little red haired girl.

Did you ever read that book "The Snows of Kilimanjaro"? This guy Harry is dying and he's thinking back on his life. He thought about all the women he knew and all the exciting stuff he did. I remember thinking to myself that it wasn't a great tragedy that he was dying. He had lived. He'd seen and done things. Death was just a final footnote on an extraordinary story.

I thought that it wasn't like that for me. I didn't do anything. I didn't leave a mark on the world. Then again, I realized that maybe I did, on you, on Cynthia, on my parents. That's all any of us can really hope for; to make a contribution to the people we love.

When I was a kid my mom was always hounding me to wash behind my ears, brush my teeth and make sure that I wore clean underwear. What made it worse was that she was always telling me to take care of myself, to look as handsome as can be. Handsome! What a joke! But she always told me that I was as handsome as a movie star. I had to brush my teeth three times a day, because that's what beautiful people do. I had to shower and have clean clothes on; I had to be presentable because the world had to appreciate how handsome I really was. I know it's every mother's job to lie to their kids that way but when I looked in the mirror, I saw the truth and every time she told me how dashing I was, I wanted to scream at her to stop, to quit lying, that I wasn't a kid who needed to be lied to.

One night, Cynthia got invited to this midnight bash that was being held at one of the in crowd's houses. Lest she should actually take her place in society, she wouldn't go unless I came along. She was always so worried about me feeling left out and I did, but it only took a look in the mirror to make me feel that way. Not getting an invitation for a party was just par for the course. But, I agreed to go, for her sake. It wasn't fair that she had to waste her Friday nights watching TV with me.

My parents were already in bed when we were leaving and just as we were heading out the door my mom appears out of nowhere in her pink robe and fuzzy slippers. "Andy, weren't you going to come kiss me good night?" After a couple "Aw moms" I went over and gave her a kiss. As she hugged me she put her hand to my neck and said, "Andy, did you have a shower? Your hair feels oily." I was inching toward the door away from her but she kept saying things like, "What kind of girl is going to dance with a boy who has oily hair?" My mom refused to accept that it would take a lot more than clean, shiny hair to get a girl to look at me, let alone move rhythmically within two feet of me. The whole point was moot anyway as the party we were going to was of the "people milling around stoned out of their minds" variety. I didn't count on a Sadie Hawkins dance breaking out at the party.

My mom said, "You're so handsome, Andy. The girls will be all over you, but how will they feel if they knew that you didn't care about them enough to have a nice shower?" I couldn't take it anymore and I really let her have it. I was standing there screaming at her, telling her that I knew that I was ugly, that she knew it too and every time she called me handsome was a smack in my face. I swore and I screamed and when Cynthia dragged me away, my mom was crying her eyes out.

Cynthia lit into me and all night, in between telling guys to go screw themselves, she was lecturing me on how terrible I had acted. I apologized and told her that I would it make it up to mom when we got back home. As for the party itself, it was a nightmare, as I knew it would be. Those who saw me wondered what I was doing there, who had invited me and did I even know how ugly I really was. For a few drunks, wondering those thoughts to themselves wasn't enough and so they thought it out loud. Cynthia gave them an earful but we left after an hour or so anyway.

I saw the red and blue flashing lights a full block away from my house. Police cars jammed the driveway leaving room for the unused ambulance and necessary coroner's wagon. I'll spare you the details, except to say that the neighbours heard the gun shots less than twenty minutes after Cynthia and I left. No need to do the math; I know all too well that if I had listened to my mom and had a shower, I would have been there when that wacko son of a bitch broke in. I might have stopped him, I might have been killed, and Cynthia might have died. Might is such an impotent word and there is no comfort or fear in it.

Do you know what stabbed me even more than the guilt? What slayed me was that I hadn't seen it coming! There I was, with this all seeing mind's eye that could pick stocks out of the financial pages and know who was going to win the next football game but couldn't forecast the death of my own parents.

Once again, I'll spare the details of the next two years. I won't tell you about the guilt, loss and above all, the anger that tempered my self-pity. I never followed the images that came to me. Visions of chance, opportunity and hope all went ignored until I found out that I was going to die. Then I realised that my ability to see things was not an inherent talent. It was a gift. Each vision came from beyond and God may not have given me the sight of my parent's death, but He did give me the vision of mine. He gave it to you too didn't He? But what could you do? What could I do?

Zachary, God chose you to be my friend. He chose you, but even if He hadn't, I would have. That night at the grocery store when I winked at you, you looked at me and saw yourself... how you saw yourself when you looked in a mirror. I got into that fight because I'd never been in one before. I never fought back against those that saw me as a pathetic little geek. Fighting back that night meant that I would never have to fight again, because I knew that it didn't matter if people thought I was ugly or weird. It just stopped being important. When you joined the fight, I knew that I'd found the best friend I would ever have. Thank you for that. What's even more bizarre, is that feeling of discovered joy wasn't the last time I felt it.

You may be shocked to learn this, but it was in Cherisse, who thought kind and gentle thoughts when she first laid eyes on me. She loved me Zachary, beyond all reason. She thought I was handsome, just like my mom did. The point is, I've lived a lifetime in these past few days. I've felt more and loved more than I ever had and even as I write these words, I'm so overcome with gratitude that God would grant me these extra days.

God calls to us all Zachary. You and I may never know the whys behind it, but all we can know is that no matter what is seen or not, we have to act. So there, now I have one more piece of advice before I continue: Answer the door when opportunity knocks...

Just then there was a knock on the door and I almost jumped out of my skin. Even as I was on my feet staring at the door in stunned disbelief I knew that Andy had written that just so he could have one more laugh at me getting freaked out.

There was a second, louder knock and I figured that it couldn't be opportunity because everyone knows that it only knocks once. I assumed that it was Cynthia, who must have forgotten something along with her key. That's why I put the letter down and answered the door clad only in the boxer shorts that Andy had bought me a million years ago.

When I did open the door, parties on both sides of the doorway were shocked. The purple underwear was enough for them but my reason was seeing Philip, the old man from the back of the limousine, two uniformed policemen and two others with badges hanging from the breast pocket of their tweed sports coats.

"Zach?" Philip gawked.

"Philip?" I sputtered.

"You! You bastard!" The old man squawked as he burst into the room with hands spread out in front of him, ready to choke me. Only one age spotted hand made it to my neck before the cops pulled him back.

"What are you doing here?" I demanded of those assembled.

"I was just about to ask you the same question!" Philip said as he stared at me with his blue tinted contact lenses.

The man from the back of the limo yelled, "Arrest that man! He's the one that kidnapped my boy!"

One of the cops that wasn't currently holding the old man back stepped forward towards me but Philip spoke up, "He can't be the kidnapper! He's from Canada!"

The same cop said, "Are you trying to say that Canadians don't kidnap people?"

Philip said, "No, I mean he just got here from Canada. He arrived three days ago with a small red headed guy and his sister. I picked them up on the highway when their car broke down."

"You don't know anything!" The old man screamed. "He was the one that took my money and told me that my son was at the Roosevelt Motel! That's the lying bastard!"

He broke free from the policemen who had let their guard down and were only holding him loosely by his suit jacket. The jacket came off in their hands and he was on me in less than a second. We both tumbled to the floor in a heap of rich old man and half naked geek. We were pulled apart quickly enough but not before I received a stinging head butt right on my... take a wild guess... nose. It was the pain and indignation which made me shout, "You stupid old fart! I didn't even know your son was kidnapped! I didn't even know those guys and I don't have your money! All I got was a lousy twenty bucks!"

The older of the two detectives said, "Wait a minute son. You didn't know which guys?"

I continued to speak in an overloud voice as blood had begun to pour out of my much-maligned nose, "The guys from the diner! Leo and Gordon and, and, the big guy! They were the ones that told me to say Roosevelt! I didn't know what it was all about! They were going to give me five thousand bucks to say Roosevelt and take the package to them! I didn't even know it was money in the bag until after I looked! Leo told me to say Roosevelt and Gordon said if the old man asks me anything to just keep my mouth shut but the big guy said to repeat it, to say Roosevelt again and... And his name was Quentin! That was it!"

The cop approached me slowly, "Now just calm down son. Take it easy, take a nice deep breath and tell me the whole story."

We all sat down except for one cop and the old man who was obviously too irate to do anything except stand there and glare at me. I told them everything that had happened from when I woke up on the beach to when Andy picked me up on the street outside the parkade.

One of the cops brought me a wet face cloth for my nose and I still had it pressed against my face when I addressed the old man, "I had no idea that those guys had your son. I'm really sorry for being involved but I know where they live and I'll help you get them."

The old man still looked grim, "All I want is to see Matthew alive and well." He paused and gave me the steeliest look, "And to see the men who did this punished."

The senior cop asked me for the address but I told him that I didn't know it. I quickly added that I did know where it was and could show them.

He nodded, "We'll want you around to identify them. That is, if they're still there and we can apprehend them."

While the cops were huddled together discussing things I turned to Philip, "So what part do you play in all this?"

He said, "I was out in Vancouver on the set of my movie for two days and when I got home there was a note in my mailbox that said, "The man who can help you crack the DeMuir kidnapping is in The Ambassador Hotel." He looked around briefly and added in a lower voice, "In this room."

I knew it had to be Andy who left that note. I just knew it. But what I didn't know was why he left it in Philip's mailbox. "But why would the note go to you?"

He pointed to the old man, "That's Elwin DeMuir, of DeMuir Pictures. The man I work for."

The cop in charge said to me, "OK, ready to go?"

I nodded and stood up, taking the pants that Philip held out to me. I put on a shirt from the top of my suitcase that badly needed a wash and then we all marched down to the cars that were waiting on the street.

Philip and I got in the backseat of the unmarked four-door police car and I directed the driver through the busy, sun washed streets. We arrived at the rundown apartment building and we cruised around the corner and back again. We parked a couple blocks away and then the cop said as he was getting out of the car, "You two wait here. Don't budge." We both nodded and then a group of plain clothed cops emerged from the urban woodwork, meeting on the sidewalk to co-ordinate their efforts.

Philip and I sat in the car trying to peer through the obstacles that barred our view of the apartment building. Across the street, in a similar car, sat DeMuir; staring eagerly at the building through the back window. We waited for a long time but nothing happened. I asked Philip for a cigarette and he gave me one out of his sleek gold case.

After he lit it for me he caught DeMuir's eye and gave him a cheerful thumbs up sign, which the old man ignored. After the voiceless snub he turned to me, "So, where is Andy now?"

"He's dead. Car accident." I said without taking my eyes off the building.

He was silent for a few minutes and then said, "How about Cynthia? Where is she?"

I looked at his smarmy face and said, "Back off Phil. Cynthia and I are engaged."

He grinned, "You got me all wrong Zach."

I said, "So you're not really a pretentious asshole?"

He chuckled, "No, I am a pretentious asshole. I mean you got me wrong about Cynthia. I could make her a star."

I rolled my eyes and took a long drag off the cigarette without answering him.

"I'm serious Zach. I could put you in the movies too. This whole thing would make a great story."

I was about to comment on his generosity for handing out stardom but just then I saw a figure creeping out from behind a dumpster. It was Leo, all arms and legs, casting furtive looks up and down the street.

"That's him!" I said as I tried to open the door and then suddenly remembered that I was in the back of a police car.

"That's who?" Philip asked.

"One of the guys!" I answered as I scrambled over the seat in front of me and dropped my cigarette, sending sparks flying off the upholstery.

"Hey! Watch it! I just got burned!"

I made it to the front seat just as Leo began to quickly walk past the car.

"Hey, what are you doing?" Philips voice was full of panic, "Get back here!"

I threw the door open and lunged out, trying to tackle Leo, who was almost parallel to the car. I was too quick and only brushed his legs, letting him take a quick side step before breaking out in a run.

I regained my balance and was after him despite Philip's shrieking warnings. Almost immediately after, Philip's calls broke off as I heard gunshots going off near the apartment building behind me. I didn't turn back to see what was happening as all my attention quickly refocused on Leo, who was only a few paces ahead of me. I took a quick breath and poured on the speed. He jumped over a pile of garbage and I was close enough to dive for his legs and when I did hit him, one of his heels came up and caught me right on the nose. I heard all the air explode out of his lungs when he hit the pavement. I fell hard too, right into a smelly pile of trash and struggled to my knees before Leo had a chance to get up. I dropped down on him and after I gave him a few punches in the nose as payback, I knocked his head against the concrete until he was too winded to offer any resistance.

Philip came rushing up, "That was great! I mean, what a shot that would be with the right director! You running down..."

Feeling blood spray out of my nose, I yelled, "Don't just stand there, get the cops!"

He turned and starting jogging back and I leaned back on top of Leo, hoping to keep him pinned until help arrived. A minute later I saw that a contingent of police were already on the way, with Mr. DeMuir taking up the rear. He had his arm around a small kid and when he arrived he offered me his hand, "Thank you Zach, they found my son and aside from living off fast food, he's doing just fine."

I took his hand and he lifted me to my feet and I said, "I'm glad everything worked out OK."

He looked over at Leo, who was being handcuffed and led away by the police. "I saw the tackle. Very impressive. Have you ever thought of being a stuntman?"

I felt a trickle of blood run down over my lip and I laughed, "Nah, I've got a glass nose."

He looked at the source of the blood, "Oh dear, it's bleeding again." He smiled, "I'm terribly sorry about my behaviour earlier."

I smiled and waved my hand, "No problem. My nose bleeds all the time."

After a brief pause he said, "So, you didn't even know about the kidnapping?"

I shook my head. "I haven't had much of a chance to watch the news since I've been in town."

"Then I'm assuming that you also had no idea that there was a reward offered."

I missed his point entirely, "No, I slept on the beach and then spent the night with my friend and then there's his sister..."

He cut me off, "It was a hundred thousand dollar reward."

I whistled, thinking of the cheque that Andy never wrote for me and then my eyes opened wider as the realisation of what DeMuir was saying hit home.

He laughed, "I'll write you a cheque at the police station."

By the time I had given my statement, collected the cheque and all the other paperwork was taken care of, it was dark outside. It was while I was at the station that I learned some of the details surrounding the kidnapping.

Apparently, twelve year old Matthew DeMuir was snatched from school two weeks earlier. The three stooges, along with a fourth accomplice were ransoming him for a cool million. The boy was supposed to be at the Roosevelt Motel the day I had met DeMuir in his limousine but the kidnappers had a sudden change of heart and decided to double the ransom. They might have got away with it if they had stuck with the original plan, but as you and I both know, greed kills. Speed too, but that's not really relevant to this situation.

When Cynthia finally made it to the station I was ready to commit a crime to get out of there. There were reporters there en masse and when I saw Cynthia we practically ran into each other's arms. One of the photographers snapped a picture and it made the front page of the Times. "A Hero's Reward" was the headline. Cynthia made a fuss over my bruised chin and bloody nose and even with the reward money and the five minutes of fame from the TV cameras, the best part of the day was when Cynthia broke off her hug and said, "Were you rolling around in trash? You really stink."

DAY THIRTEEN

Friday the Twenty Third

Remember how I told Philip that Cynthia and I were engaged? I was ready to use that lie on anyone who came within drooling distance of her. Firstly, to scare people off, but also because it was the kind of fib that felt so good to say. It felt so good that I wanted it to be true. I know what you're thinking; we had only known each other for a total of thirteen days. Yes, I knew that, but I was madly and deeply in love with her. Moreover, by all accounts, she felt the same way about me.

I suppose it was a safe enough proposition to make. I mean, we live in the age of people being engaged for twelve years or the more socially acceptable, "being engaged to be engaged." The only flaw with that blow softening idea was that I was thinking about all of that on the cab ride through Las Vegas, which is the four minute wedding capital of the world.

My fear quickly shifted from, "She'll say no for sure" to "She'll say yes and we'll be man and wife before suppertime." If she was anywhere near as impulsive as her brother, we would be sharing the reception with the Elvis impersonators, pregnant showgirls and drunken gamblers who married the girls who blew on their winning dice.

I knew that I would have to be very careful in how I popped the question. It had to be romantic and heartfelt enough to get an answer in the affirmative but it also had to be solemn and mature so she wouldn't want to do it within the next couple of hours.

"What are you thinking about Zach?" Cynthia's sweet voice pulled my mind back into the cab.

"I was just wondering if you would marry me."

How's that for romance and solemnity?

I saw the cabdriver look back at us in the rear view mirror and smile, even though he probably heard more wedding proposals than Pamela Anderson at an autograph session.

Cynthia smiled and held my hand, "OK." Then she looked out the window again.

I sputtered, "OK? You'll marry me?"

She smiled, "Well, not today or anything. But yeah, let's do it."

Was she perfect or what?

The cab stopped in front of a small pink house on a quiet residential street that would have fit right in any town except Las Vegas. I mumbled something like that and Cynthia looked at me like I was the stupidest fiancé she ever had. "Did you expect the house to have neon signs in front?"

Thankfully she didn't wait for my answer, which would have no doubt been something asinine. "I guess this is it." She said after a quick breath.

"Do you want me to go in with you?"

She shook her head, "No, we already went through this. You go see Bobby and then we'll meet back at the airport." She leaned over to me, "Now kiss me for luck."

"Good luck." I said, and kissed her.

She got out of the cab and quickly walked past the brown and unruly lawn to the house. I told the cabby to wait until the door had been answered and when Cherisse appeared at the doorway I told the driver to go. I closed my eyes and saw Andy, a little drunk and a lot in love, kissing Cherisse at the roulette wheel. The night he defied Las Vegas odds seemed so long ago.

When my cab ride was over I looked up at the unlit sign in front of the Ozone. I had two hours to break the news of Andy's death to Bobby Fabian and get back to the airport. I figured that it wouldn't take long with Bobby, as he probably wouldn't even show that he cared. It just wouldn't be his way.

It was Cynthia's idea for me to see him, arguing that it was the right thing to do. I was just happy that she had volunteered to tell Cherrise, the one who was bound to be emotional. I remembered the way that she looked at Andy when they walked out of the restaurant on the outskirts of town. It was the look of a woman in love.

Even though I felt calm about telling Bobby, I still took a deep breath before I pulled the doors open and went inside the deserted bar. Bobby was sitting at the piano, dressed in shiny mauve pants and a purple sport shirt, both made of some alien, likely toxic, material. He was playing a really nice melody that didn't match his attire or his style. It wasn't until two months later, when Cynthia was trying to "impart some class" by playing me classical music, that I realised the tune Bobby played was written by Chopin.

I made it all the way to the stage before Bobby noticed me. "Zachary! You dog!" He hopped off the stage and gave me a hug, "How are you? Where's that freak, Andrew? Out robbing the casinos before it's even dark?"

I looked into his smiling, bloodshot eyes and decided to make it fast, "Andy's dead."

He blinked, slowly, and took two steps back.

"It was a car accident. Three days ago."

He turned around slowly and climbed the stage steps toward the piano. He picked up his grey silk-like jacket and slung it over his shoulder. He looked around the empty room, wiped a tear away quickly and then looked back to me, "Got time for a drink?"

"Sure." I said with a nod.

He put the jacket on, adjusted the collar and tucked his shirt in. "Let's go someplace that has... what did Andrew call it?"

"The Vibe."

"Yeah, The Vibe. Let's go someplace that has The Vibe."

As soon as we were outside Bobby took his jacket off, "The nights are great in Vegas, but the days are brutal."

I nodded, looking down the street absentmindedly.

He sighed, "But I love Vegas no matter what."

We walked down the strip but didn't even pause at any of the casinos. Without a word, we slowly ambled all the way to the end of the strip and then Bobby stopped, turned to the entrance of a glitzy hotel and said, "How about this one?"

I shrugged, "Fine."

We ordered drinks from a passing cocktail waitress. I had a ginger ale since it was barely noon and Bobby had a double scotch, neat. When our drinks came he took a large sip and said, "Poker and craps are my games. I noticed that Andy didn't play poker."

"Too slow, he said."

"Yeah, too slow."

"So, craps then?"

He shook his head, "No, I already told you craps is my game. I always lose at my games." He took another sip and motioned to a blackjack table, "There. We'll play over at that table."

We each got twenty bucks worth of chips. Bobby made a ten-dollar bet and won. I lost my twenty on one hand and then smiled as I thought about all the twenty and fifty dollar chips that were still in my tuxedo jacket. "I'll save them for next time." I thought as I watched Bobby play. He won the next five hands and had a nice little pile of chips in front of him. Neither of us spoke, not wanting to jinx his run of luck.

After finishing my second drink, which was, incidentally, a root beer, I looked at my watch and said, "Bobby, I gotta get going."

He nodded, barely noticing as he busted after a hit. We shook hands, "Y'know Zach, Andrew didn't die. He's here, somewhere in Vegas, making long shot bets and winning every one of 'em."

"Maybe." I said.

"No maybe about it. He's here. Guys like Andrew don't die. They just keep winning."

"You may be right Bobby. Take it easy."

He said, "Oh hey, where's the love of my life?"

I smiled, "You realize that you're talking about my future wife." It felt good saying it and knowing that it was true. I guess I must have looked pretty pleased with myself and Bobby pointed to my face, "You've got some root beer on your lip."

I wiped it off quickly, "Thanks."

Then, without any warning, Bobby hugged me and I could see the tears glistening in his eyes when he let me go. "Come and see me sometime. We'll hunt for Andrew together. Even if we don't find him, maybe we can drain the coffers and start another legend."

"We'll do that." I said with a smile.

I left Bobby at the blackjack table and took a cab to the airport. I was a little early so I took a seat near a window and looked out at the city and desert that lay beyond. The noonday sun cast harsh rays down on the brownish yellow landscape, making heat ripples rise. I thought about Andy, dying in the desert night and of his shell, sitting in refrigerated storage back in L.A. I missed him terribly, turning my eyes back to the city that would light up people's hopes along with the night sky.

I could see Andy at the tables; red hair glistening, gap tooth mouth grinning and tiny freckled hands clutching chips. I saw him laughing, hollering and stuffing those chips into his pockets, my pockets, and Cherisses' purse. Never again, and my heart ached with loss.

Bobby had lost the legend of a little guy who robbed Vegas and lived, at least for a little while, to tell about it. Maybe Bobby figured that it was the odds, rising up in monstrous form and coming to exact vengeance on the white tuxedo-wearing hero. It was that cruel hand striking the insolent boy who defied the rules, the indelible laws of chance. Maybe it was more; maybe Bobby had simply lost a friend.

As for Cherisse, if love did indeed beat true under a low cut blouse, then her loss would be the greatest of us all. One day was all it took for her to see magic. Love, without its usual costume of good looks and standard approach. Love, which came in a tiny, ugly package, and burned a hole into a heart long hardened under the Vegas sun.

I mourned again, and not only for myself, but also for Bobby, who was alone, and for Cherisse, who unwrapped a gift only to have it taken away. Thankfully, the mourning did not last long as I saw Cynthia at the other end of the terminal. She was walking slowly and looking around so I stood up and waved to her. She saw me almost immediately and came straight for me. I didn't have to ask her how things had gone as it was plain to see that she had been crying. We were in each other's arms without a word of greeting and we stayed that way a long time. In fact, when the boarding call came, we were still holding each other tightly.

"She collapsed right to the floor when I told her." Cynthia finally said as the plane levelled off at twenty thousand feet. "She cried and beat her breast. She was a total wreck and she only stopped when her daughter woke up. Even then, as she held Andrea, she kept telling me how much she loved Andy and how she had planned the rest of her life around him." She dabbed at her eyes with a tissue and then smiled, "When I die, you better mourn for me like that."

I didn't smile, "Don't even joke about it. You're all I have in the world."

"You're all I got too." Then she kissed me on the cheek and cleared her throat, "So, what happened with Bobby?"

I said, "I honestly didn't think it would hit him, but he actually allowed a tear."

She smiled, "Probably the first one in twenty years."

"Nah, he's a really sensitive guy." I said, "He probably cries every time a woman shuns him."

She laughed, "Nobody can cry that much."

"Hey, don't be mean. Bobby was Andy's friend."

She grabbed my hand suddenly as the plane hit an air pocket and then said, in a shaky voice, "I know that, Bobby loved Andy too."

I felt my hand cramp from the pressure she was applying and I said, "Next time we go to Vegas we're driving."

She nodded gratefully, "Andy would want it that way."

When the plane landed in Edmonton, Cynthia and I were both yawning although it was barely suppertime. We had to hang around for another hour because of a luggage mix up and when we got it all sorted out, caught a cab and finally pulled up to Cynthia's house, now hers alone, we were both jet lagged to such a degree that we leaned on each other as we walked.

The house was musty and seemed like an empty cathedral. Cynthia was yawning to beat the band, and said during one of the breaks, "Want some supper?"

I smiled, "You go have a shower and I'll fix us up something to eat."

She took my hand and kissed it, "Now you sound like Andy." As she started for the stairs she turned to me and said, "And thanks, you're an angel."

While she was showering, I rummaged around in the kitchen and came up with a couple cans of tomato soup. It was steaming in the bowls by the time she came downstairs and she laughed when she saw me standing there, wearing Andy's poofy chef's hat.

"Don't I look dashing?" I asked with a big grin.

She smirked, "Wicked."

She took the hat off as she kissed my forehead, "Your turn to shower after we eat."

I said, "I think I'll head home after supper."

She looked shocked, "What? You're not staying here tonight?"

I smiled, "I haven't been home in almost two weeks. I have to see if all my invaluable junk is still intact. With your permission I'll come back tomorrow."

She frowned, "Permission granted, and you better bring your invaluable junk with you because I'm not letting you go anymore."

During supper I told her of my plans for spending deMuir's reward money, which included paying off my odious student loans. Cynthia smiled as she twirled her spoon in the soup, "And where do I figure into your monetary plans?"

"I'll take you to Macdonald's every day for a week."

She laughed and fluttered her eyelashes in a coquettish fashion, "Oh my, the benefits of having a wealthy fiancé."

We cleared up the dishes together and then she gave me the keys to her BMW. "If you aren't back here at noon I'm having you arrested for grand theft auto."

I left my luggage in the foyer because I would be back well before noon. Just as I was going out the door Cynthia told me to wait and then rushed off. She came back in under two minutes holding the plastic grocery bag that held razor blades, deodorant and toothpaste. All the things that run out at once when I have to go out and face the rest of humanity. Inside the bag were the reasons that I went to the grocery store in chapter one. I looked at it strangely for a moment before taking it from Cynthia. Then, a quick embrace and sweet kiss and then I was gone, driving a silver BMW westward, and a little to the right.

The sun was setting when I put my key in the door and I stepped right into a sunbeam once inside my apartment. I looked around and thought how the last time I was there I didn't even know Andy. The last time I sat in my chair, the last time I used the toaster, the last time I slept in my bed, Andy didn't exist in my sad little world.

I went to the window and looked down at the grocery store parking lot. I imagined the fight we had; Andy's bloody shirt and the black Mercedes parked a few stalls over. How much could he have taught me if he had lived? What joy could he have brought me? What other things could he have said?

Suddenly, with that last thought barely out of my brain, I remembered his letter and I panicked as I thought I had left it in the hotel room in L.A. No, I had packed it. No, I hadn't. I put it in the pocket of my pants. Those pants were packed, in the suitcase, back in the foyer at Cynthia's house. "Damn," I thought, "It'll have to wait."

I went over to the table and picked up the grocery bag but when I grabbed it, I only had one handle and the contents spilled out onto the floor. What caught my eye was the yellow box of chocolate covered raisins. Somehow, they ended up in my bag. I picked them off the floor and then I saw the letter. Placed there, no doubt along with the chocolates, by Cynthia. I took the box and the letter over to my chair and started reading.

"Answer the door when opportunity knocks...

Well, all things sorted out now? Don't be mad Zachary; I needed to freak you out one more time. I know the above was supposed to be my last piece of advice but I think I have a few more parting pearls. Remember to sing in the shower, always have dessert, have a skip in your step, take the time for sunsets and sunrises and live, live, live each day as if it were the last. And oh yeah, enjoy married life. I have a feeling that the Tiernans aren't done with you yet.

Your friend,
Andy

PS: Enjoy the chocolates. They're the best chocolate covered raisins in the city!

I set the letter down reverently on the coffee table and popped a handful of chocolates into my mouth. I watched the sun dip below a building and let out a long sigh. I stood up, stretched, and smiled. Then I had a shower.

A special message to you, my dear Reader:

First of all, thanks for buying my book. I hope you enjoyed it. If you did, can you do me a favour and tell a friend or two (or fifty)? When you tell your friend about this book, tell them that it radically changed your life, and then they'll be more inclined to buy it. That's how marketing works apparently. When they read it, they'll get this message too. Then they can tell fifty more people and so on and so on and voila, I'm on Oprah!

Now that we've shared so much of each other's lives (well, I have... you really haven't shared anything with me. You should work on that) feel free to send me a note on Facebook (if Facebook still exists by the time you read this) and let me know that you liked the book. If you didn't like it, then let's just keep that to ourselves, shall we? No one likes a complainer.

Thanks again,

Frank

Made in the USA
San Bernardino, CA
08 April 2017